"Mirroring the great short stories by Raymond Carver, *Two Syllable Men* will appeal to both men and women. McCaffrey's use of dialogue to plum the rich internal worlds of his characters is uncanny, and his modern take on the age-old battle of the sexes reveals a soulful poignancy."
JILL DEARMAN, AUTHOR OF *THE GREAT BRAVURA*

"Down, but not out, the men of John McCaffrey's *Two Syllable Men* are as complicated as they are conflicted: not to be reduced to the sum of their two syllables. Wounded by loss and longing for love, they may feel compelled to lie, cheat, steal—or simply charm—to conceal their vulnerability, yet aspire to so much more. McCaffrey's twelve stories here are astute case studies of the human male, finely nuanced with pathos while undeniably hilarious."
TIM BRIDWELL, AUTHOR OF *SOPHRONIAL.*

"With the rhythmic precision of a prose poem, *Two Syllable Men* charts the interiors of twelve remote men in or around love. John McCaffrey writes with a musicality that's rare in literature today."
IRIS SMYLES, AUTHOR OF *IRIS HAS FREE TIME*

"It makes sense that this book opens with a quote from Pablo Neruda: master of writing odes to simple things that end up encompassing all of life. McCaffrey does that too. His stories are filled with the sensory: beige heels, bacon fat and peanut butter sandwiches, ATM receipts, kickboxing, sex on boats, yoga, the office. You feel bad for these characters, but you also relate to them. The men in these stories represent aging and growth, and sometimes the refusal to do either. McCaffrey's stories are easy to read, but they give you things to think about for a long time. He makes embarrassment and loneliness so real that it's almost uncomfortable. He proves that people—all people—have layers of complexity. And really, at the end of the day, all we need is someone to eat a meal with."
MICAH LING, AUTHOR OF *FLASHES OF LIFE*

"John McCaffrey is a writer who thinks carefully about what he has to say, then chooses his words deliberately and wonderfully well. He's insightful, literate, funny and wise. Read these stories! They're finely-crafted gems!"
BURT WEISSBOURD, AUTHOR OF *THE COREY LOGAN TRILOGY*

ABOUT THE AUTHOR

John McCaffrey grew up in Rochester, New York, attended Villanova University in Philadelphia, and received his MA in Creative Writing from the City College of New York. His stories, essays and book reviews have appeared regularly in literary journals, newspapers and anthologies. His debut novel, *The Book of Ash*, was released in 2013. He lives in Hoboken, New Jersey.

Visit *jamccaffrey.squarespace.com*

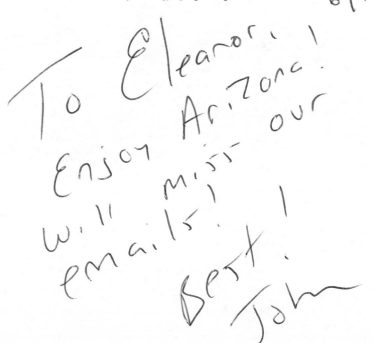

6/17

To Eleanor!
Enjoy Arizona!
Will miss our
emails!
Best!
John

Print Edition
ISBN: 978-1-925417-10-4

Published by Vine Leaves Press 2016
Melbourne, Victoria, Australia

This is a work of fiction. Any similarity between the characters and situations within its pages and places or persons, living or dead, is unintentional and co-incidental.

Cover photography from chechotkin, shock
Cover design by Jessica Bell
Skyline designed by Freepik
Ohm symbol designed by Scott de Jonge at flaticon.com
Interior design by Amie McCracken

National Library of Australia Cataloguing-in-Publication entry (pbk)
Author: McCraffrey, John, author
Title: Two Syllable Men / John McCaffrey
ISBN: 9781925417104 (paperback)
Subjects: Short stories
Men—Psychology—Fiction
Dewey Number: A821.4

TWO SYLLABLE MEN

John McCaffrey

Vine Leaves Press
Melbourne, Vic, Australia | Athens, Attica, Greece

TABLE OF CONTENTS

"I want to see the thirst
inside the syllables
I want to touch the fire
in the sound:
I want to feel the darkness
of the cry. I want
words as rough
as virgin rocks."
—Pablo Neruda

WILLIAM

IT IS IN HER apartment, with her gone for pizza, that William finds himself alone and prying. Looking around and admiring her tastes, her choices in furniture, her decorative abilities. It is a geometric apartment. All angles and edges. She is an accountant, and the home speaks of economy and order. But it is also soft. The colours warm, dark, with bits of highlights. Like her, he decides. He likes her things. Her leather couch. Television. Computer. He feels comfortable in the space.

On an end table, near the couch, William sees a spiral notebook. He flips it open. It is filled with words. English words. His native tongue, not hers. The script is military precise yet dainty, light, the ends of letters punctuated with upturned curls. Next to the English word is its Chinese equivalent, and then, in English again, the definition. He scans the words, pages of them, and begins to see a pattern. The words, at the end of the notebook, the most recent entries, were spoken by him.

The first one is *possessive*. It is almost scratched into the paper. There is no curl at the end of the *e*. William mouths the definition: a desire for ownership, occupancy, hold. The word *hold* is underlined. He traces it with his finger and flushes. He remembers the conversation. Just days earlier, on the phone. She had questioned his whereabouts over the weekend. Doubted the veracity of his claim that he was with friends. Accused him of infidelity. "Some young girl," she spat out, her accent thick. He said she was crazy, that she was being possessive. He remembers the silence on the phone. Thinks: was she jotting down the word?

After possessive is *resolve*. The word is stretched on the page, the *o* oblong, the *v* wide and flat. She has written out two definitions. The first: to break up into separate elements or parts. The second is written all in caps. It says: TO MAKE A DECISION ABOUT, TO MAKE CLEAR. William winces. He has been using the word constantly with her. Always in reference to his pending divorce. Justifying why he has not pushed it through faster, why he still talks to his wife, "the woman," as she describes her, "who left you."

"I'm just trying to resolve things," he had said, over and over to her. "I need to resolve some issues before I move on."

William's head tightens. He flips a page. Sees the last word entered: *content*. It is written so faint he has to hold the page up to his eyes to make out the definition: happy enough with what one has or is; not desiring something more or different. He smiles. Thinks of the night before. They had gone to a movie. And then back to her apartment. They had undressed each other. Played. Danced and wrestled their way to the bedroom. Then, on her low-lying bed, they kissed. And he was flooded with joy; it ripped through him. He had gripped her bare shoulders. Licked at her skin, off-white and flawless. Gripped tighter and tighter; absorbed her body. Later, as they lay sated, he looked at her and said: "I feel so content."

He closes the notebook and walks to the lone window in the apartment's living room. He looks out and across at another building, sees people behind curtains, near sinks, in bedrooms, getting dressed, watching television, talking. He hears the door of the apartment crack open. She walks in, pizza box in hand. She sets it on a table and removes her coat. She smiles and looks at him. William walks toward her, searching for the right word.

DANIEL

DANIEL WAS checking out a woman. She was tall and stylish in a beige mini with matching heels. Her brown hair was done up in a bob that exposed small, round ears. Her pale skin was clean of makeup, intensifying her green eyes. She flashed them at Daniel as he arranged a box of soft tofu into her grocery bag.

"Can you put that in plastic? I know paper is better for the environment, but it will soak right through."

Daniel did as asked. When finished, he scanned the other cashiers to see if they needed his service. No one was busy and so he stayed put.

"Will you carry these to a cab for me?"

Daniel scooped up the bags and followed the woman. Once at the curb, she looked left at the ongoing traffic and raised her arm.

"I've met you before," she said, still focused on getting a cab. "Melony Harper. We grew up in the same town."

Daniel was not sure she was speaking to him. In the City it was common to see people talking to themselves, either because of some mental oddity or into a concealed mobile phone.

She turned to face him and lowered her arm.

"You were in the same class as my older sister, Lauren."

Daniel finally made the connection. He remembered Lauren Harper to be attractive, smart and funny, exactly the type of girl that intimidated him. He hardly ever spoke to her growing up.

"She's married with two kids already, if you can believe," Melony added.

Daniel fidgeted uncomfortably. He did not like being away from the register, did not want to upset his boss and risk a bad review, something that would be sent to his parole officer and the manager of the halfway house. It was not admonishment that concerned him, but attention. Basically, all he wanted from the job was the paycheck, all he wanted from the halfway house was the bed, and all he wanted from the supervisors in his life were signatures on the documents that kept him free and out of prison.

"What about you? Married?"

"No."

"Me neither. Have you lived here long?"

Daniel knew to the minute how long, as his move to the City co-incided with his release from jail. It had been exactly 45 days since he was processed out and placed in the home. Still, he shrugged his shoulders as if unsure.

"I've been here two years," Melony said. "But it seems like forever."

Daniel couldn't wait any longer. He stepped forward, and hugging the groceries to his chest, managed to raise his right arm and flag down a taxi.

Melony opened the cab door and slipped inside. She took the groceries from Daniel and smiled.

"Thanks," she said. "I hope we can catch up some more another time."

With that she closed the door and the cab moved back into traffic.

His boss didn't reprimand him, but still it was an unpleasant evening for Daniel. There was a stirring inside him that altered the way he had felt since leaving prison. He had been living in a state of ambivalence, a cocoon of uncaring that kept him moored to the program set out for ex-convicts, allowed him not to question the path of mediocrity he was expected to travel, not to complain about the decrepit environs, the sinful wages, the crushing isolation of the societal miscast. That night, however, he longed for more: a nicer room, new clothes, money in his pocket … a woman in his bed.

Work was hectic the next day. A sale on vegetable oil drew in a slew of food cart vendors. Bagging the oil wore him out, and with relief he took his first break and went outside for a smoke. There, to his surprise, he saw Melony.

"You too," she said in greeting, exhaling gray fumes through her nostrils. "I thought I was the only one left who smoked."

Daniel blushed, suddenly aware he was holding a dingy plastic lighter and a cheap pack of cigarettes. Before prison he smoked Dunhill International Lights. What he liked most was the packaging, the square, sophisticated shape of the box, the slick red and egg-shell white colouring, the neat script across the top and the gold inlay, like holiday gift paper. But a carton of Dunhill's would devour his pay, and so now he smoked Winstons, which came in a dank-looking pack encased in flimsy plastic.

Daniel extracted a stick and stuffed the pack back into his pocket. He lit it fast and secreted away the lighter.

"It's nice out today," Melony said. "But I heard it might rain later."

Daniel dragged hard on his cigarette.

"I don't mind rain," she continued. "It doesn't make me feel guilty to stay in bed."

Daniel inhaled deeper, willing the lit end to draw closer to his lips.

"I was going to see if you have time for coffee," Melony said, dropping her cigarette and grinding it out with the heel of her shoe. "I mean, after your shift."

Daniel cringed. He hated the word—shift. Only poor people worked *shifts*.

"I'll understand if you're busy."

He wasn't busy. And the idea of having coffee with Melony excited him. Not because of sexual attraction, but more for the attention it might bring—the envy he perceived in the eyes of other men when he once made it a habit to stroll into restaurants and clubs with a beautiful woman by his side. He thought that this desire to impress, to be bigger than his life, had been blunted by his two years in prison, the degradation of incarceration and the slow tick-of-time acting together like a giant mirror pressed to his face, forcing him to be humble, to examine up close his imperfections. But instead of blackheads and scars, wrinkle lines and in-grown hairs, he saw fear and weakness, indecision and insecurity, a man without purpose or identity, a man stripped of his mask, a façade erected out of bluster and bravado, ruthless largess, abject greed … and stolen credit cards.

"I can."

He was as surprised by his answer as Melony seemed to be. She made a move for another cigarette, fumbling with the pack as she pulled it out from the handbag over her shoulder.

"That's great," she said. "What time?"

Daniel had to think quickly. He got off at eight but had to be inside the halfway house by 10 each night. Off all the rules, and there were many, this was impressed upon him from the start as the most essential to maintain. If broken once, it meant a reprimand, a call to the Parole Officer, and a note in the file. If broken twice, it meant expulsion from the house and, possibly, a return to prison. He'd already broken curfew once, in an act of rebellion even he didn't quite understand, when one night during that first week at the house he purposely stayed outside, smoking his cheap cigarettes, waiting until after 10 to knock on the locked door and take his punishment. He was determined to not let any more urges, conscious or subconscious, jeopardize his freedom.

"How about we meet right after eight," he finally said, trying to project a casual unconcern about time.

"That works for me."

Melony finally got a firm hold on another cigarette and lit it.

"Do you have a favourite place?" she asked, pushing smoke out of the side of her mouth. "If not, I can suggest something."

Daniel glanced to his left. Half-a-block away was a small café. He had never been inside, taking his morning cup of coffee at the halfway house and the rest at the market.

"That's where I hang," he finally said, indicating the spot with a nudge of his chin.

"Perfect." Melony blew more smoke into the heavy air. "So I'll see you tonight."

Daniel affirmed the plan with a nod, and after Melony left he returned to the store, where he waited at the end of Lane Five for the mid-day crush.

Inside the café was dainty looking, the interior painted a bright yellow, with streams of purple paisley stripping the top and bottom walls. The chairs and tables were tiny; more suited for children than adults. In contrast, the earthenware coffee cups were huge, like soup bowls. Daniel picked up his with two hands and took a hard swallow while Melony spoke.

"I feel so complicated lately," she said, pausing to blow into her cup to cool the coffee. "It's like I crave simplicity, but I have no idea what that even means anymore. It used to be that I could wake up in the morning and plot out my whole day—pick my meals, where I was going to go, who I was going to meet, even what I was going to feel like. I'm sort of into visualization: if you can see it you can be it, that kind of thing. So if I woke up and saw myself smiling, I would smile. But lately, when I wake up, I have no idea what I want to feel, and so I spend the day going from one feeling to another, which wouldn't be bad if most of them were positive. Does that make sense?"

It didn't, but Daniel nodded anyway.

"Good," she breathed with relief. "I thought I was going crazy. I actually thought about going to a psychologist, but they cost a lot of money and I don't have insurance. Besides, from what I hear, the only thing they do is medicate people, and I hate medication. I won't even take a vitamin."

Daniel took another hit of coffee. It tasted oddly sweet, but it packed a caffeine punch. In prison, the coffee was watered down and weak, probably because they didn't want to give the inmates any more reason to feel edgy or over-stimulated.

"I think it comes from my father," Melony continued. "He's very rigid when it comes to what goes into his body. It drives my mother crazy, because she likes to cook with fat. I'm not lying. She makes bacon every morning, and saves the grease and uses it the rest of the day. She even smears bacon fat on peanut butter sandwiches."

Melony wrinkled her nose.

"Do you ever miss being home?"

Daniel eyed a clock on the back wall. It was just past 8:30. He figured another half-hour and he'd leave, putting him back at the house in time to have a smoke before curfew.

"I guess ... sometimes."

"I'm the same way," Melony said. "Like when I'm mad, or down, nothing looks good. But when I'm happy, everything is gorgeous. I can see the worst thing, the saddest thing, like a homeless person in the rain, and if I'm happy, I'll find something nice about the scene. Like maybe the homeless person is making a conscious choice to be on the streets; that they want to be free and not tied down by any big money needs, like paying for rent."

Melony paused, shot a sad look into her cup.

"I don't think I told you, but I came here to work for a friend who opened up a vintage dress shop. No one bought the dresses and the store's closing."

She looked up.

"Are they hiring at your market?"

Daniel blushed, embarrassed to be reminded of his menial job.

"It's probably a bad idea," Melony answered her own question. "I'm sure it's a great place to work, but I think the best thing for me is to go home and lick my wounds. Or at least swallow my pride. That's my biggest problem: I have too much integrity. I can't stand dishonesty or anyone who is a phoney. It's not a good trait for retail sales."

Melony finished her coffee.

"Can I get you a refill?"

"I've had enough."

"Not me," she said, "I'll be right back."

But there was a line at the counter, and when Melony returned it was already nine.

"Sorry it took so long. But I'm happy to see lots of customers. It was really sad about the store I worked. Do you mind if I tell you about it? I really haven't had a chance to talk to anyone about what happened."

Daniel gave another look at the clock. He guessed he could wait another five minutes and still make the door. But the cigarette was out. He'd have to risk smoking it in the room, another violation if caught.

"Sure," he said.

Melony began talking. First, she told him about the store; how excited she was to get the job, how she thought the vintage clothes and accessories—"hippie, bell-bottom jeans and lots of funky beads"—would sell well, and how this excitement, this hope, was tamped down little by little each day, as fewer and fewer customers came through the door, and even fewer, once entering, actually purchased something. Soon it became apparent the place would have to close, and with it the end of her job, but she could not find the energy to start over, to search for a new position, to go through the whole process again of finding an "employment partner," as she called it, telling him that she never wanted to just "work somewhere just to work," but to actually care about the business, the products, the people involved.

By the time she finished, the five minutes had turned into ten. If Daniel was to make the door, he would have to excuse himself immediately, rush from the table, sprint to the subway, hope a train was coming, hope it would make all the connections without pause, and then, if he ran hard from the station to the halfway house, he might, barely, make it.

But he stayed. Listening and eyeing the clock as Melony switched topics at random, often with no natural break or segue to warrant a change in subject, speaking for one moment about her love of lemon ices to watching a documentary on Greenland sharks. She also told him about her favourite flower—"Lilies, because their stems curl forward like a giraffe drinking water"—and her most hated, black-eyed susans, because her last boyfriend cheated on her with a woman named Susan and she was not yet ready "to forgive him or her."

By now it was nearly 10:30, and a worker at the café was mopping up the floor. Melony had gotten a third cup, and Daniel, resigned to his fate, had allowed her to get him a refill as well.

"I guess we're closing the place," she said, laughing.

Daniel's mind was stuck on the closed door of the halfway house, his empty bed, the whispers among the other residents about his absence, the manager angrily filling out the report, making a note to call his parole office in the morning.

"Can I tell you something?"

"Sure," Daniel returned.

Melony's expression changed, the set of her mouth and eyes sticking somewhere between concern and compassion.

"I know you were in jail. My sister told me when I told her I had run into you. I'm just telling you because I don't want you to think you need to hide it from me. And you don't have to tell me anything about it. I talk a lot, but I also know that it's good sometimes to keep things in, to let a hurt keep hurting until it doesn't hurt anymore."

Daniel waited for a wave of embarrassment to overtake him, but it did not come. Before jail, if anyone, especially a woman he was with, hinted at anything about his character or past that was not positive, he would react with a manic flurry of words to prove her wrong. But now, sitting in the closing café with a last cup of coffee, he realized that he did not care what Melony thought about him. The feeling was liberating, and buoyed by it he took her in as if seeing her for the first time, sizing her up with the sharp eye of the seasoned con man, and not the struggling convict.

"I got to go," he said.

Melony's face fell.

"I knew I shouldn't have brought it up. I upset you."

"Far from it. I just got things to do."

Daniel pulled out his wallet and opened it. He had inside a ten dollar bill and three ones—the rest of his money until payday. He pushed onto the table the ten.

"For the tip," he said.

Melony seemed more confused than hurt.

"You really got to go?"

"Yes."

Daniel was already moving past the table. His plan was to walk the streets a bit, maybe hit a few bars—not to drink, but to check out the customers, the drunk ones, the ones who absently left billfolds on the counter, credit cards and slips. He would stay out until dawn, and then head back to the halfway house. He had heard rumors that the manager could be bribed to look the other way now and again. He would try to find out. With luck he would avoid be written up, could take a quick nap, and then a shower and shave, and back to the market. Lots of credit card slips there for the taking.

"Wait," Melony said. "I'm here a little longer … maybe we can meet out again."

Daniel turned and shot her his best smile, one he hadn't used since before prison.

"Sure," he said. "But this time we'll go out for real: nice restaurant, drinks, music and dancing … my treat."

"Are you sure? It sounds expensive."

"Don't worry," he said with a wink, thinking to himself that tomorrow he would also pick up a pack of Dunhills and a new lighter. "It's only money."

GRAHAM

I BOUGHT A bottle of beer and sat next to a woman I found attractive at the bar. She was alone and reading a book. I finished the beer and introduced myself.

"Graham," I said. "Like Graham Greene."

The author's name didn't register any emotion, but she did shake my hand when I extended it and told me she was Meg. She was reading *The Sun Also Rises* and I asked her about Hemingway. She said she preferred Fitzgerald and we discussed *The Great Gatsby.* I bought another beer and a rum and coke for her. When Meg finished the drink and got up to leave I asked for her number. She seemed sincere as she wrote it down on a napkin, but when I called the next night I got an airport limousine service. The operator told me no one named Meg worked there.

A few weeks later I spied a great looking blonde in a halter top at the same bar. She was dancing in place near the jukebox and I imagined for a moment she was a French harlot from a Maupassant story and I was a lecherous Count. I downed a tequila shooter and introduced myself. Her name was Claudine and we found common ground talking about writers and books. It turned out she really liked Jack London. She also liked tequila. After a few more shooters she said I would look good in a parka and snowshoes. I agreed and made a move to kiss her. We had sex that night and started dating.

Things were good in the beginning with Claudine, but by our second month together I sensed her interest waning. Trying to stem the tide, I bought her a hardcover copy of *The Sea Wolf.* It didn't help. She kept the book and broke up with me.

The next few weeks I lived at the bar. I pined hard for Claudine, writing love poems in my head and doodling pictures of her face and body on napkins. I thought several times of going to her apartment and trying to win her back, but a mixture of pride and cowardice kept me rooted to alcohol.

One night, deep in a funk, I met Talia. She was taller than me and approached with a shot of Jim Beam in each hand. She gave me one and we talked. I learnt she played basketball for a local college women's team. She was also an English Major. When I asked her favourite author she didn't hesitate: "Somerset Maugham." She spoke for an hour straight about his work. I found her passion erotic and suggested we go somewhere more private to talk. She must have sensed my real purpose because she told me she had a rule never to have sex with a man until he watched her play basketball. She said her next home game was in three days.

I marked my calendar and waited. But right before I was to leave for the game Claudine rang me. She said she had been reading Jane Austen and was feeling romantic. She thought now I would look good in aristocratic clothes. I told her I had a tweed jacket with denim elbow patches in my closet. She asked me to put it on and come over. I did.

A few weeks later I was at the bar when Talia tapped me on the shoulder. "You never came to my game," she said. She pulled a book out of a knapsack and passed it to me. "I've been holding this for you. It's *Of Human Bondage*. Maugham's best."

"What's it about?"

"Read the book." She pantomimed shooting a basket. "Then come see me play."

Claudine and I continued on a good patch for another month before it fell apart again. It coincided with her new interest in Gertrude Stein. She even quoted Stein's *Stanzas in Meditation* in a grammarless letter explaining her reasons for breaking up a second time.

I fell into another drinking depression. I brought *Of Human Bondage* to the bar and began to read it while I downed shots. I was moved by the story of a man who fights to break free from the hold of passion an abusive woman has over him. The day I finished the book I looked up the schedule for Talia's team. They had a game that night. I got there early and bought a ticket not far from the court. The two squads came out and I spotted Talia in the lay-up line. She looked sexy in her uniform and knee pads. I stood and shouted her name. I got excited when she turned and looked into the stands. But then I realized it was someone else that held her attention. He was standing a few rows below me. He was tall and skinny and was wearing a jersey with her number on his back. And in his hand, which he waved with joyous frenzy, was a book.

KEVIN

"What's your name again?"

I took a pull from my Jack and Ginger, making sure to wince as I swallowed.

"Kevin."

The old man on the stool next to me nodded. We were talking and drinking at a bar I walked into that morning. It was now past five in the afternoon.

"I'm Clay," he said, his lips parting to reveal a neat row of lime-white teeth. "But don't try to mould me."

I laughed once, and then returned to the Jack and Ginger, performing a full grimace as I drained it.

"Still smarts?"

"Something awful."

My pain wasn't all phoney. I was hurting from my wife walking out on me. That was the *real* extraction. The other, about having a wisdom tooth pulled out, I'd made up. It was an excuse to get off work and drink, and I'd decided to carry the lie around with me the whole day.

Clay siphoned off the head of a new beer.

"You say your lady took off?"

"Last week."

"Sorry to ask, but is she shacked up with another guy?"

"No," I said, "her sister."

"If she's not with a guy, then you still have a chance. Call her up and say your mouth is sore and you need her to take care of you. I bet she'll come back."

"I doubt it. She hates me."

"So what. Women aren't like men: they can love someone they hate."

I didn't want to talk anymore about my wife, so I brought up his.

"I can't believe what you told me. I would've called the cops on her."

"I almost did."

"What stopped you?"

"I guess I thought that if she was willing to do all that to get my attention, it was worth giving it to her."

"And things worked out?"

Clay finished his beer. He smacked his lips with satisfaction.

"Better than I hoped."

The bartender came over. He lifted away my empty glass and mopped up underneath with a hand towel.

"Another?"

"Sure," I said. "And a beer for my friend."

Clay held his right hand up.

"No more for me. I got to get home for supper."

"Just one."

"Can't do it."

"Your wife must be a good cook."

"She was," Clay said, "before she passed."

"I'm sorry. I didn't know."

"How would you?" Clay blew out his cheeks as he exhaled. "It might sound silly. But even though I'm alone, I like to sit down at my own table and eat dinner every night. I even set out a plate for her. If I don't, I feel adrift. Know what I mean?"

"I think so."

Clay rose from the stool and nudged his chin toward the bartender who was busy making my drink.

"Your next is on me. Tell Jeff I'll square up tomorrow."

Clay left and I scanned the bar. Only a few customers remained, all men, each intently watching a horse race on the overhead television. Underneath the television was a jukebox, unplugged and dull with dust. The flooring consisted of chipped checkerboard tiling. The metal stools were covered in black vinyl littered with cigarette burns.

"You're Jeff?" I asked when the bartender returned.

"That's right."

"The old guy that just left, Clay, said to put this on his tab."

Jeff held the drink in his hand.

"Is there a problem?"

"You need to pay for it," he said flatly.

"Why?"

"Because he's a bum."

I pushed over a ten-spot.

"He seemed like a good guy."

"He's not."

I didn't like Jeff's quick putdown.

"You should cut him some slack," I said. "His wife's dead."

"Who told you that?"

"He did."

"Well, she's alive."

"You sure?"

"I hope so, it's my mother."

"Clay's your dad?"

"Stepfather."

Jeff took my money to the register. He came back and stacked the change, five single dollars, next to my drink.

"Look," he said, "don't take it personally. Clay lies to everyone. That way he doesn't have to be himself."

He moved down the bar and began working on the other customer's refills. I finished my drink and walked out. It was dusk and coldish. I thought about what to do next. It occurred to me that I better go find some dinner. Then again, chewing food might hurt too much with the extraction I'd endured. It felt good to lie, even if only to myself. I turned and went back inside and ordered a drink. A new race on television had begun.

BYRON

AFTER HIS wife left him, Byron tried to blunt his loneliness with obsession. The first was automated banking machine receipts, which he would scoop up off the floor or out of wastebaskets at 24-hour banking centres, bringing them home and laying them out on his kitchen table, as if he was readying a deck of cards for a game of concentration. Then he would pour out a glass of wine and begin the deliberate process of scrutinizing each slip, imagining the people who owned the accounts, if they were a man or a woman, what they looked like, what was their job, how they spent their money, if they were married or not—fantasizing, speculating and dreaming late into the night, until the bottle was drained and so was he, ensuring that falling to sleep, difficult since the breakup, would come easy.

One day, he discovered a new obsession. It was bound to happen: the receipts, after a time, began to lose their ability to excite him, to transport him out of his own reality; eventually, the scenarios he concocted grew dull, even depressing, until he was no longer wondering what people were doing or not doing with their money, but why they needed money at all. He began to creep into a bitter melancholy thinking about the uselessness of it all, about working and saving and buying things, about the terrible differences in wealth, how the entire society was drowning in thoughts of money, in bits of paper spit out of mundane machines that measured their value, defined them.

And so Byron flirted with the idea of becoming a Communist, or at least immersing himself in Communist doctrine. His idea was to buy some books on the subject, and in the spirit of the endeavour, and because money was tight, he snubbed the monolithic chain bookstore in town and headed to a used book bazaar in the basement of a Protestant church. His intention was to purchase anything written by Marx or Trotsky, even Mao, something red and dusty and revolutionary. The best he could find was a short story collection of Gorky's, a hardcover that smelled of moth balls as he flipped through the pages. He was surprised to find, wedged near the middle of the book, a postcard.

On the front was a photo of a scantily clad woman, her arms wrapped suggestively around a street lamp, her face hidden behind a Venetian mask, her voluptuous breasts sequestered in a white T-shirt with the words *Bourbon Street* emblazoned in hot pink letters. He flipped over the card, read what was hand-written in a purple pen: *Arnold, You are not missed. Nor will you ever be. Sabina*

Byron paid two bucks for the book and went home. This time he laid in bed as he examined the postcard, studying the photo, sniffing the paper, psychoanalyzing the handwriting, visualizing Arnold and Sabina, pondering their relationship, his mind drifting to all the possibilities behind their seeming rift, until his eyes closed and his body, both excited and sated, found sleep.

Byron began to haunt the bazaar on Saturdays, the only day it was open, spending hours pulling books from the shelves and out of cardboard boxes, rifling fast through the pages, shaking them by the spine, sifting through them like a miner panning a stream, looking not for gold but leave-behinds, intentional or accidental bookmarks, business cards and restaurant menus, grocery lists and faded photos, folded dollar bills and recipes, debris from a past reader's life, evidence that someone else had been there before him, fuel to transport him out of his existence and into another's.

One afternoon Byron was walking home from the bazaar with a new purchase, a hardcover copy of *The Sun Also Rises*, which, perhaps because it was missing the cover, he found in the fifty-cent bin. His desire to own it, however, was near the end of the book, between pages 184 and 185, to be exact, amidst the passage when Brett leaves Jake, Robert Cohn and the rest of her party of ex-pats in Pamplona to pursue an affair with a young and dashing bullfighter. There, tucked tight to the spine, was a square white envelope, the kind used to respond to wedding invitations. It was yellowed with age at the corners and sealed with red wax shaped into a tiny heart. The envelope was not addressed.

Byron's usual method was to wait until he got home to study his bookmarks, but his excitement about what may be inside the envelope got the best of him, and as it was a pleasant late summer afternoon, sunny, but not too hot, he decided it preferable to head to a local park and open it there. He chose a bench shaded by a towering elm, old enough that its trunk was wider than the bench was long, and bald in spots where the bark had been ripped off and replaced with graffiti markings speaking of unrequited love and individual existence. He sat down with his back to the sun and opened the book, flipping through the pages until he reached the envelope. He was about to pull it out when a tall, lithe woman passed by, stopped, and then walked swiftly over to the bench.

"Wendell."

"Excuse me."

Her face, long and plain without makeup, congealed with confusion.

"Aren't you Wendell?"

"No," Byron said, startled by the abruptness of her approach and question.

"I'm sorry. You look like someone named Wendell I met once."

"It happens," Byron said, recovering his senses.

"You mean other people have called you Wendell?"

Byron blinked. He was not sure if she was joking or not.

"You're the first."

"I imagine people mistake you more for a Robert," she said. "Or maybe Leonard. Something with two syllables."

"How come?"

"Just the energy you give off. You seem calm. People with two syllable names are always calm. At least that's my experience."

"Thanks."

"So I'm right?"

"Sort of—my name's Byron."

"After the poet?"

"Actually, my father."

"Was he a writer?"

"No, a welder."

The woman squinted at his hands.

"What are you reading?"

Byron had forgotten the book, the envelope, his reason for sitting down.

"Oh, this." His mind drew a blank on the title. He looked down, but without the cover, the only thing facing him was a blank page. He turned it over to the back where a description was posted. "*The*

Sun Also Rises. Hemingway. I just bought it." He turned it back over, pointed to the blank page. "Used."

"That's good. No need to buy something new when you can get it old."

She smiled.

"Mind if I sit down?"

Byron blushed. Since the split with his wife he had not been close to another woman, emotionally, intellectually, or physically—navigating around them with caution, as if they were underground landmines.

"It's just I've been walking all day," she continued.

Byron slid over so that his right hip pressed tight against the bench's arm.

"Certainly," he said. "There's room."

The woman sat down. Byron hadn't noticed she was carrying a backpack, a black mesh satchel with braided straps that looped over the shoulders of her brown T-shirt. She removed the satchel and set it on her lap, so that the material spread over her khaki shorts, nearly to her knees. Byron blushed deeper, thinking the mesh sexy against her long, shapely legs. He also liked her feet, which were slender and exposed in open-toed sandals.

She rummaged inside the bag and pulled out a plaid-coloured thermos.

"Would you like some water?"

"No thanks."

She removed the lid and took a sip. Waited, and then took another.

"Perfect," she said, screwing the top back on and returning the thermos to the bag. "I put cucumber slices and mint leaves in my water. They have natural cooling properties, you know. I drink that all summer and I'm never hot."

Byron forced his gaze from her legs to her face, realizing now it was not so plain. Her eyes, in particular, were peculiar in shape and colour—perfectly round and inky black, with sparks of white at the edges. They reminded him of photos he had seen of solar eclipses.

"I might try that sometime," he said. "I sweat quite a bit."

He regretted the statement immediately. It was not attractive to sweat, he thought, certainly not to talk about it.

"Well, you can also soak in the mixture," she said. "Just add Epsom salts with the cucumber and mint. That's what I do—sit back with a glass of wine and lay for hours in the bath before bed."

Byron felt as if his ears were going to burst, he was blushing so hard. He turned away and coughed into his hand.

"Are you okay?"

"Just something in my throat."

"Are you sure you don't want water?"

"No thanks."

They were silent a moment. Byron found the break in conversation uncomfortable, and scoured his brain for a suitable topic to keep it going.

"Do you live nearby?" he asked.

"Yes. I let a room in a house next to the church across town."

Byron held up the book.

"That's where I bought this."

"That's right," she said. "They sell books in the basement. Do you go often?"

"Lately."

"You must be an avid reader."

Byron paused a moment before answering.

"More I just like books; I mean, what's inside of them."

"That's cool. You can learn a lot about yourself from reading."

Byron took in a deep breath. His wife, before they split up, often criticized him for being too passive, accusing him of being a counter-puncher in life, someone who reacted rather than initiated. He remembered their first date, when he asked if he could kiss her, and she surprised him with an angry response, explaining that a man never asked to kiss a woman, he just did it.

He blew out a stream of air.

"Maybe we could meet there sometime?" he asked, trying to sound nonchalant. "It's open Saturdays. We could look over the books and take a walk after—come back and sit here if you like, or go get a coffee."

Her face grew serious.

"Do you mind if I ask if you're single?"

"No. I mean, yes. I'm separated."

"Children?"

"No."

"Are you trying to get back with your wife?"

Byron hesitated.

"I'm not judging you if you are," she continued. "It's just that I have this thing where I'm attracted to solitude. It's like an obsession. I'm drawn to men who are comfortable being alone. I found that there are two kinds: one type likes to be alone because they like to be alone; the other is forced into solitude by loss. I've failed in relationships with both kinds. The men who like to be alone didn't mind being with me now and again, but they couldn't make any meaningful commitment to a relationship, as that goes against their loner DNA. And the men who are isolated because of loss, once the pain goes away, once they get back on their feet, lose the need for solitude and want to be social again, sometimes to excess, which, for me, is a turn off. So I break up with them, causing them a similar pain that they just got over."

She nodded her head as if reinforcing a painful truth.

"So I have a problem. I don't want to get hurt or hurt anyone."

Byron smiled. Her revealing made him feel more confident.

"I take it then you're single?"

"Hopelessly," she laughed.

"And your name?"

"Didn't I tell you?"

"No."

"Emily."

Byron smiled.

"Do people with three syllable names have a personality trait as well?"

"Good question. I'd say we're unfinished. We need one more beat to become an even four—to become complete."

"You sound like a numerologist."

"More like obsessive compulsive. But I'm working on it."

"So want to meet next Saturday? How about noon?"

Emily stood. She looped the satchel over her shoulders and smiled.

"Two is better."

"Okay. Two."

Byron lingered on the bench after Emily left. He could not believe he had just asked a woman he barely knew on a date, and more that she had accepted. After some time, he returned his attention to the book in his hand, to where the envelope was quartered. He pulled it out and fingered the wax seal, the tiny red heart. He was about to break it open when his eyes caught on a sentence on the page:

Together we walked down the gravel path in the park in the dark, under the trees and then out from under the trees and past the gate into the street that led into town.

Byron finished the rest of the passage. He suddenly had a desire to become immersed in the words, to get lost in the action, in the lives of the characters, to be drawn into the fantasy, not create it. He slipped the envelope back into the fold and flipped to the front of the book. There was still plenty of light to read by. He began with the first sentence.

STEVEN

"Hot today," Steven heard.

The sound of her voice ignited an erection—the soft hiss of her *h*, the guttural spike of the *t*, the languid flutter of the *y*. Steven turned to the woman across the narrow aisle on the commuter bus. She was short and petite, her small breasts accentuated by a crisp, white cotton T-shirt. Steven had never experienced such visceral lust for a woman at first meeting. She wore a knee-length denim mini, which offset smooth tan legs, and her tiny feet were fitted snug into a pair of smart leather clogs. Her eyes were the colour of coal, and her sandy-brown hair shone like wheat in a sun storm. She had a long, freckled nose and cheekbones sharp enough to cut glass.

"Yes," he returned, "it's very hot."

"They say it might break tonight, but that's what they said yesterday for last night. I just hate living in air conditioning, don't you?"

Steven was conscious of the purplish discoloration under his eye. He'd gotten the wound a few days earlier, after slamming into a shabbily dressed woman pulling a grocery cart filled with strips of coloured fabric. The collision didn't cause the bruise—the woman's bone-thin fist did. With one swing she dropped Steven to the bus station's sooty floor. "Don't try to steal my cloth," she screeched. "I know you want my colours."

Steven raised his hand to his face, hoping to obscure the mark. "Air conditioning is horrible," he said. "Though I have to admit I sleep with a small window unit right over my bed. I always wake up with a stuffy nose."

He wanted to hit himself. A stuffy nose: what was he thinking? But the woman did not seem turned off by the statement.

"I understand totally," she said. "Do you get a sore throat as well?"

"Sometimes I can barely swallow until lunch."

She smiled knowingly. "Sandy."

"Right. My throat gets sandy—all rough."

"No," she said. "My *name* is Sandy."

"Oh, sorry," he blushed. "Steven. I'm Steven."

"It's you."

Steven whirled around. He hadn't seen Sandy since their introduction on the bus, and he had been kicking himself for being too scared to ask her out at the time. That's what confident, cool, successful single men on Wall Street did, he figured. He was a trader of stocks and bonds and was surrounded by volcanic machismo each day. If one believed everything said on the floor, then not only was the New York Stock Exchange the centre of the financial universe, but also home to the greatest collection of sexual conquistadors the planet had ever known. Steven felt inadequate in this raucous world of ribald men, but it was the only job he'd ever held, inheriting his seat on the exchange from his father.

"Hey," Steven said, his face turning crimson. "How are you?"

Sandy wiped a blonde bang away from her eye. She was wearing a light pink sleeveless blouse and matching skirt. An enormous handbag of nearly the same colour hung from her shoulder.

"I'm good." She patted the bag. "Got my gym clothes inside. I usually go straight from work. If I go home first, forget it, I'll just sit in front of the television and eat junk food. Don't get me wrong, it's still sitcoms and chips most nights, but at least I feel less guilty if I work out first."

"You look great," Steven said. "I mean, you don't look like you eat too much."

"Thanks, I think."

"What I mean," he said, trying to save the moment, "is that you look quite fit, like you really take care of yourself."

"Going to the bus?" Sandy asked.

Steven shook his head up and down.

"Follow me."

Steven trailed a foot behind Sandy who spoke over her shoulder as they walked.

"I'm actually taking a kickboxing class tonight," she said. "Have you ever done it?"

"No, but it sounds like fun. You know, kicking people."

"I guess. I'm not naturally aggressive, but I need an outlet for my job stress."

"What do you do?"

"I'm a lawyer," Sandy said. "Corporate stuff. And you?"

"I'm a trader."

Sandy slowed until Steven couldn't avoid striding next to her.

"That's great," she said, gently grabbing his elbow and guiding him around a puddle of what looked like coagulated strawberry milk. "I can always use investment advice. Can we meet for a drink sometime and talk?"

"Sure," Steven said. "I can go out with you—I mean talk."

"So let's pick a date. Let me check my calendar."

The collision was perfect. As Sandy was reaching into her bag, Steven took a wide step to his left and buried his shoulder into the man's chest. He was husky, red-faced, and wore a cowboy hat. He was solid. Steven's shoulder popped out of its socket, and then a piercing pain set in. He stumbled to the floor and lay flat on his back. After a few seconds he passed out, Sandy, phone in hand, staring down at him.

The ad in a local newspaper read:

FEELING OUT OF CONTROL?

I CAN HELP

NO MEDICATIONS, NO PSYCHOBABBLE,

JUST PLAIN, TOUGH TALK

KIMBERLY GOTBEIN, PH.D

Steven skipped taking the bus and walked to Dr. Gotbein's office, located a few miles from his apartment in an industrialized section of town. She held sessions inside a mobile home, a double-wide trailer set amidst a gravel lot littered with discarded tires and rusted hubcaps.

Dr. Gotbein greeted Steven wearing a soiled pink muumuu.

"Hurry in," she said, frown lines creasing the sides of her mouth. "I got the air conditioning cranking."

Steven sized her up with a glance. She was grossly overweight, with ankles as thick as telephone poles and so much poundage around her neck that when she talked it looked like waves of fat were rolling toward him. Still, there was something oddly attractive about her. Maybe it was her hair, which shone a curious purple-black, with a subtle curl at the bangs. She also had wonderful eyes, a smoky blue that contrasted brilliantly with her dark hair. And she was light on her feet, twirling around like a ballet dancer while sweeping Steven into a chair at the kitchen table with a nudge of her gargantuan forearm.

"Would you like a snack?" she asked. "I have cold fried chicken in the fridge, some leftover macaroni salad, and fudge brownies a patient baked for me yesterday."

"No thanks. I'm not hungry."

Dr. Gotbein scratched her forehead.

"Typical. Men with problems never eat; women with problems eat all the time."

Steven consciously breathed through his mouth. The trailer smelled like rancid cooking oil and mothballs.

"So," Dr. Gotbein continued, "what's your problem?"

It was freezing in the room, and Steven was wearing only Bermuda shorts, open-toed leather sandals, and a thin blue T-shirt. He shivered before speaking.

"I'm cold."

"Emotionally vacant, huh. Disinterested in life. I've seen a lot of that lately."

"I mean, right now. It's freezing in here. Can you turn down the air-conditioning?"

Dr. Gotbein shook her head. "Sorry, this is the only temperature that holds off my hot flashes. So unless you want to see me naked and sweaty, suck it up and start talking."

Steven exhaled with resignation.

"Okay. I guess ... I mean ... you see ... "

"This is like a bad blind date. Do I have to guess what's eating at you or are you going to spill the beans?"

"Sorry," Steven began again. "How to say this? Best to be succinct, right? Okay, I guess you can say I've been bumping into people inside the bus station."

"I would say being succinct may be one of your problems, but the other thing ... in the bus station. I should be so lucky. I never bump into anyone, except for my patients. All my friends are either retired, in Florida or dead ... sometimes all three."

"I didn't explain it right. Bumping into ... I mean, I've been, for lack of a better word, crashing into people. Strangers, that is."

Dr. Gotbein furrowed her eyebrows. They were thick, dark, and connected.

"So you're doing this on purpose?"

"I suppose. I mean, I don't want to, but I can't stop myself. An urge overtakes me."

"And this is how you hurt your wing?"

Steven nodded. The incident with the red-faced man had resulted in a separated shoulder. Sandy had gone to the hospital with him where the doctor in the emergency room popped the joint back in place and wrapped the whole shoulder in a sling. Steven had been taking pain pills ever since. It was finally starting to feel better.

"And the bruise on your face?"

Steven nodded again.

"How long has this been going on?"

"For awhile."

Dr. Gotbein bit at her lower lip.

"Any of the doctors who patched you up check for anything else?"

"No, just fixed wherever I got hurt."

"Like what?"

"Before the separated shoulder, two broken fingers, a broken rib, and some stitches here and there."

"And not once did they give you a CAT scan?"

"No. Why?"

"Maybe you have a brain tumour that's screwing with your equilibrium?"

"A brain tumour?"

"It's possible," Dr. Gotbein said. "Listen, I had a patient once with erectile issues. He thought it was because of his wife's tendency to leave the room whenever he got naked, but it was actually physical. The poor sap had a growth in his prostate the size of a meatball."

"Why are you telling me this?"

"This is serious business. I don't want to waste your time if you're terminal."

"I had a physical not long ago. I was okay then."

"Now is not then. But let's say, for arguments sake, that you're not dying, that you're really just losing your mind. Have you ever spoken to anyone else before?" She dug a sausage-thick finger into her left nostril. "You know, a qualified mental health professional."

"Yes. A few years ago."

Steven's experience in therapy came after another trader blew his head off with a shotgun when the Dow dropped forty points in one day. The Exchange hired a grief counsellor to speak with anyone having trouble coping with the tragedy, and Steven took the opportunity to meet with a therapist each day for a week during his lunch break. He enjoyed the sessions and was disappointed each time he had to return to work. What he liked most was the chance to talk to someone without being interrupted.

"Did it help?"

"Sort of, I guess. But I never talked about this. I mean, other than what's happening in the bus station, I'm pretty normal."

"Listen, you don't seem well adjusted, and psychosis doesn't happen overnight. It's like weight gain: you don't get obese on one double cheeseburger, but five a day, for three years and it's time for the gastro-bypass."

Steven's heart raced. He gasped and pressed a palm against his rib cage.

"I don't feel good," he said.

"More the reason to get moving on this."

"I'm not sure."

Dr. Gotbein patted Steven's hand. Her touch was warm and moist.

"Listen, it's normal to feel nuts. Once you accept that, everything will work out. I'm not saying you have to be bananas to feel good. But you won't feel good if you can't feel bananas. Understand?"

Steven didn't, but his panic began to recede.

"So do you want to continue or not?"

Steven exhaled through his nose, wondering what he had to lose.

"Sure," he finally said. "But first can I have a brownie?"

"I think it's great you're seeing a psychologist," Sandy said.

Steven pushed the phone receiver into his ear. He had not thought to tell anyone about Dr. Gotbein, but somehow he could not resist opening up to Sandy. They had talked on the phone every night for a week since the collision, usually before bedtime, and Steven had revealed to her many of his anxieties and worries.

"I got some counselling during college," she continued. "It was after I caught my first real boyfriend in bed with my roommate. I actually forgave them both. But right after that I started to throw myself at any guy I saw. I was shameless, brazen, letting them have sex with me any time they wanted—anywhere they wanted. It was only after I did something really bad that I went for help."

"What'd you do?"

"That part of the story will have to wait until you know me a bit better."

"Would you like to have dinner with me tomorrow?" he blurted out quickly. "I could cook for you at my place."

"Sounds fun. Should I bring something—wine, beer, dessert?"

"Just yourself," Steven said, unsure why he volunteered to cook, considering he hadn't made a real meal on his own in years, subsisting mainly on restaurant takeout, frozen dinners, or a simple sandwich.

"It sounds too easy. You sure no strings are attached?"

"Well," Steven mumbled, embarrassed by the risqué turn the conversation had taken, "you helped me get to the hospital. So I should repay you, right?"

"Steven," Sandy said like a scolding teacher. "It's okay to like me. I like you."

Steven's face burned crimson. Thank God she can't see me, he thought.

"So I'll see you tomorrow night at my place. Seven is good, right? Or eight. Or six, if that's better. I'll call you tomorrow and set a time. I mean, you can tell me what time is best."

"Steven," Sandy said before hanging up, "you're funny."

Dr. Gotbein cleared her throat of barbeque pork. The shredded meat oozed out of the bun, covering her knuckles but not reaching her fingertips. It took Steven by surprise that Dr. Gotbein ate during sessions, not being shy about speaking with her mouth full, rocketing half-eaten bits of food at his face when she became impassioned about a topic.

Steven cringed as he unconsciously voiced the same word that had sent her into a half-hour, egg salad-spraying rant during their previous meeting: "Distance."

Steven tried to pull the word back as soon as it left his mouth, but almost immediately a chunk of pork hurtled past his right ear.

"You need distance?" she said. "You've slept with the woman once. You think she wants to marry you? You're that good in bed?"

Dr. Gotbein's disparaging remarks toward him were commonplace. It was only their fourth session, but he was already used to the abuse.

"I didn't mean that," Steven said. "I just don't want to give Sandy the wrong impression. I'm not ready for a close relationship."

"I thought it was my high blood pressure, but it's you that's killing me. The problem is you are ready, and the whole thing is screwing with your head."

Steven chewed on his lower lip. He hadn't seen the point in much Dr. Gotbein had said in their previous sessions, but since they had begun working together he hadn't had the urge to smash headlong into anyone.

Dr. Gotbein finished the sandwich with a large bite.

"You've reached a saturation level," she said, her voice muffled by the food. "Your conscious self doesn't want to be alone anymore, so it's making a power move. And your subconscious is fighting back with both barrels."

"You make it sound like war."

"It is," Dr. Gotbein said. "Ever study military strategy?"

"No."

"A winning army always has one thing going for it."

"What's that?" Steven asked, leaning forward.

"Ruthlessness."

Dr. Gotbein dug an index finger into her back molars and yanked out a lodged piece of pork. She stuck the finger back into her mouth and sucked down the morsel with a loud swallow before finishing.

"And you, my friend, don't have it."

Steven's morning started with a message from Sandy, delivered to him by the same slick-eyed delivery boy who brought the traders coffee, candy bars, aspirin, antacids—any beverage, snack, or pill that would help amp up their energy or dull their pain during a normal, chaotic day on the floor.

"Envelope for you," he said, his face oozing from fresh-squeezed blemishes.

Steven pulled a crumpled dollar from his pants pocket for the kid and fingered the square envelope at its edges. He worked the tip of his thumb under the seal and popped it open without ripping the paper. Inside was a sparkling white card with a green and yellow dandelion embossed on its upper-right corner. The note was handwritten in faint blue ink: *Steven, I want you tonight. Love, Sandy.*

Two hours later Steven noticed a major upswing in textile stock purchases. Usually, he would go with the flow, inch money into the buying stream, secure a safe number of shares with methodical caution, trailing behind the main thrust of activity like the tail end of a comet. Rarely did he take time to deduce the impetus for the buying or selling, try to uncover the nexus, the rationale behind stock surges or dips. Instead he just followed or retreated based on the activity of other traders. This time, however, his brain locked onto an idea, the words of the strange woman with the cart rang through his head: "Everyone wants my colours."

When the bell rang to end the trading day, Steven could not believe the risk he'd taken. He'd sold his entire portfolio, liquidated all of his assets, and used the proceeds to buy shares in a string of companies that performed fabric-dyeing services for major fashion lines. To bet like he had was a huge gamble that took guts and daring and a bit of craziness. On the subway ride to the bus station he kept thinking that he surely would reap riches if he was right or lose his seat on the Exchange if he was wrong. No matter the outcome, he felt exhilarated that he'd made such a bold move.

Steven bobbed his head side-to-side like a prize-fighter as he sauntered into the bus station. He'd called Sandy right before leaving work to say he also wanted her. It excited him even more when she lost her breath at his directness.

Steven had no idea what had come over him, why he suddenly felt swift and sure of himself, manly and tough, like an outlaw predator ambling into a dusty town. He thought about buying ribbed condoms as he walked toward his gate. Maybe even one of those prophylactics that came in raunchy packaging—wrappers with *Bareback* and *Thrust* written in big black lettering on their covers. And instead of wine he considered getting a bottle of Scotch, or maybe even Irish whisky—something strong that would roll over ice with a snap and loll in a clear glass like a cocky hoodlum.

"Watch out."

Steven never saw the scooter. Its left front tire rolled atop his right foot and stopped. The old man guiding the machine slammed a bony fist into the steering wheel.

"Son of a bitch."

Steven could feel the bones in his toes flatten, spread, readying to splinter.

"Back up," he pleaded. "You're on my foot."

The old man leaned over and stared down at the tire.

"You move."

"I can't," Steven breathed. "I'm stuck."

"Well, I'm not moving," the old man said with venom. "Why should I?"

Steven was light-headed. Tears welled in his eyes.

"Please," he said. "It hurts."

"Admit you walked in front of me. Admit I didn't hit you on purpose."

"Yes, it's my fault."

"Now you can't sue me."

The old man hit a lever and the scooter careened forward, clipping Steven's shin in the process. His toes immediately throbbed. He hobbled to the gate amidst the stares of others waiting in line.

"You should go after him," a short woman with a beehive hairdo said. "That old creep hits everyone. I've seen him do it before. You should go after him and get his name and sue him. I bet that old creep has money."

Steven shook his head. The foot was numbing.

"No," he said. "I should've watched where I was going."

The lady had a face like a crow, with small black eyes that angled toward her pointy nose. And like a bird pecking at road-kill, she moved her head backward and forward as she talked.

"He veered right at you. You should get a policeman and file a complaint. Let me tell you, if he ever ran into me, I would let him have it back in spades."

She balled a fist and shook it at Steven.

"You see, I don't take any crap. Someone wrongs me, I wrong them right back. Don't you get it? You have to be tough to survive."

"What happened?" Dr. Gotbein snorted as Steven limped into the trailer on crutches. "I thought we had the thing beat."

Steven grimaced as he bent down into his usual chair at the table. He rested the crutches against the back wall, and then stared down at the plaster cast on his foot.

"It wasn't my fault. Some old guy in a motorized scooter ran over my foot."

Dr. Gotbein studied Steven with a wary eye.

"Were you in the bus station?"

"That doesn't matter. I didn't want it to happen. I didn't even see him coming."

"You sure?"

"I'm positive."

"Strange that someone hit *you* in the bus station. It's ironic, don't you think?"

"Maybe I deserve it for all the times I hurt other people."

"You hurt yourself most, it seems." Dr. Gotbein settled into the chair opposite Steven. "All those times you smacked into people, they never got injured like you did. Why do you think that is? Given that you nearly broke your own body to bits."

"I don't know."

"It's not complicated. I'll let you in on a secret: your problem isn't special. Maybe your particular dilemma in the bus station is unique, but basically it's the same garbage I've been dealing with for years."

"Just tell me then," Steven said, anger causing him to bite off his words. "You think you're so smart."

Dr. Gotbein slapped the table.

"That's the first time you ever showed some real emotion here. I'm proud of you."

Tears welled from the corners of Steven's eyes. He turned his head and wiped them away with a whisk of his hand.

"Don't get too keyed up. What I'm saying about not being special is good. It means you can be fixed. You should be thankful. I've had too many walk through this door that have no hope. There's just no way they can make it."

Steven thought he saw Dr. Gotbein's round face soften.

"What are you looking at?" she said with a snap.

"Just waiting for you to tell me why I never hurt anyone when I hit them."

"You tell me."

"I don't know," Steven said. "That's why I pay you."

"Pay me. You think I need money? I don't need money. I just charge what I charge to make it worthwhile to the patients. You get something for free and it means nothing. You pay for something and you want something back."

Dr. Gotbein changed her tone, like a schoolteacher encouraging a slow student.

"Tell me why you don't hurt anyone you bump into?"

A shadowed image of Sandy's silhouette popped into Steven's mind.

"I'm fragile."

"Wrong."

Steven's throat tightened.

"I'm unlucky."

"Even more wrong. What did I say about being ruthless?"

"I'm not."

"Correct. Now tell me why you only hurt yourself when you bang into people."

Steven closed his eyes. Sandy began to draw clear of the shadow. She was smiling, her lips pursed and glistening, her eyes eager.

"I don't want to get hurt."

"Keep going."

Tears leaked from Steven's eyes.

"I pull back right before I hit them. I clench up to protect myself."

"Bingo." Dr. Gotbein drummed her thick fingers on the tabletop. "Another axiom of war: an army that doesn't go full bore always takes the most punishment."

Steven's cheeks were slicked with tears.

"I don't know why I'm crying," he exhaled.

Dr. Gotbein leaned back in her chair.

"Because you finally connected with what's inside you. Trust me, that's the hardest hurt in the world, finding out who you really are."

It'd been a week since Steven had taken his do-or-die position in the market, and the stocks he'd acquired had not moved up or down in that time. He also hadn't seen Sandy. She'd phoned several times to meet, but he'd shrugged her off with different excuses. "You know where you can reach me," she said before hanging up the last time she called, a tinge of resentment in her voice he hadn't heard before.

The kid messenger nudged Steven in the back. It was near the closing bell, and Steven had again watched his stocks sit still for an entire day.

"Another envelope for you."

Steven tipped him and opened the envelope. A whiff of cream cheese filled his nostrils as he pulled out the letter inside. It was from Dr. Gotbein.

Dear Patient,

You owe me $75 for the last session. Draw it out in cash and give it to the first person you see on the street that you want to give it to. We won't be seeing each other anymore, I've decided. If you still feel like smacking into someone, go all the way. Remember, nothing good in life ever comes if you do it half-assed.

Cheers,

Kimberly Gotbein, PhD

Steven tossed the note and envelope onto the trading floor. He glanced up at the board and saw that textiles were still surging. His stocks, however, were dropping. When the day's trading ended, and after he calculated his losses, he found he could just make his margin call. But another day's losses would surely break him.

He trudged off the floor and onto the street. He decided to walk the forty or more blocks uptown to the bus station. It was surprisingly cool after weeks of torrid weather—a gentle breeze lifting the heavy city air away and replacing it with a crispness that helped ease the tension in his body. The sky was blue and cloudless, but the sun's light was tinted with a mysterious gray that generated a soft, exotic aura. Steven moved in measured steps as his thoughts wandered from Sandy to his position in the market.

"It's you."

The words pulled Steven from his internal meditation. He turned and stared at the woman he'd rammed into just weeks ago. She was standing next to the same cart, but it was now empty of fabric and filled with an assortment of empty soda cans.

"For a long time I was mad at you for crashing into me like that." She raised her left arm and pointed a bony finger toward the sky. "But then God told me why he sent you. I understand now that you were just following orders."

The woman startled Steven by slamming her right palm against a crumpled soda can wedged into a corner of the cart.

"See, I thought God wanted me to collect those colours," she said. "But I was wrong. He sent you to wake me up." She rapped the can again. "Now I'm collecting tin. On a day like this, with so much good sun, my cans reflect positive light into me all day. That's pure love, baby. God's powerful shine."

Steven remembered Dr. Gotbein's note. He dug into his pocket, pulled out his wallet, and extracted seventy-five dollars.

"This is for you."

"What's that?"

"Money."

The woman looked around with quick turns of her head before snatching the bills.

"I hope it'll help you."

The woman ignored Steven, counting out the bills and then stuffing them into the opening of a can she pulled out of the cart.

"Maybe you can buy some food or something."

The woman dropped the can into a soiled pocket of her dress.

"What's that?"

"The money," Steven said. "I hope you can do some good with it."

"What money? You never gave me anything."

Steven nodded his head. "You're right," he said. Then walked away.

The urge to crash into someone, anyone, obliterate them, separate them *limb from limb*, as the cliché went, dripped from Steven's pores. The desire swept up from his feet and coursed through his arms and stretched into his fingertips. He felt mean and vicious, vile and cruel. He had never felt this way before his other collisions. Then, an acute emptiness, a numbing hollowness, a feeling he'd never really been able to fully describe to Dr. Gotbein, would take over his psyche. It was almost like a crushing realization of his loneliness and isolation overtook him, and the only way he could free himself of the dread, at least for the moment, was to smash headlong into another person.

This feeling, however, was alive. It first bubbled up in the morning as his stock position hit rock bottom and his one-man company, his family seat on the Exchange, was officially lost. He left the floor at lunch and didn't return, sitting on a park bench and staring out across the murky brown Hudson River. He waited there until near dark, until the sun dropped behind the horizon—before he rose and headed to the bus station.

As Steven walked, he thought about what Dr. Gotbein had said, that the hardest hurt in the world was "finding out who you really are." Now he knew she was wrong: the hardest hurt, he decided, was having others see this truth. Letting them see that you're not good enough, not smart enough, not desirable enough. Letting them see the ugliness and reject you for that ugliness. That was the hardest hurt.

Steven swung open a door into the bus station. But Dr. Gotbein was right about one thing: doing something "half-assed" never got anyone anywhere, and he was living proof. He was finally going to barrel into someone at full steam. He moved forward with quick, long strides, searching faces for the right person to crush.

He spotted Sandy. She was walking with head down, her hands rummaging through the giant gym bag. Amidst the din of shoes and sneakers and boots clacking and smacking the tiled floor, Steven could hear her heels alone, a sharp click that tickled his ears. She closed in fast, coming right at him as if dragged by a taut rope. He began to walk toward her, narrowing his vision until she alone appeared in his sight line. His whole body was afire. Sandy was the one. He smiled and prepared for impact. He would connect with her his own way, he decided.

RONALD

THEY WERE in a downtown café drinking Chai Lattes. Her name was Alice and they had arranged the get together after meeting on an online dating service. She took a sip from her drink and then spoke fast, laying out her story in two breaths. She was thirty-one, a Duke graduate, a communications major who grew up in Virginia but loved living in New York City and loved her job for a public relations firm. She enjoyed sports: Duke basketball, of course, and NASCAR racing. She was looking for a man who was quiet but fun and liked to laugh and take walks on the beach. And what about Ronald?

Ronald coughed, sipped his coffee, and winced at the heat. It was his first date since his divorce nearly a year earlier. He had been boning up for the event for days, reading *Dating for Dummies* and poring over back issues of men's magazines. The suggestions and tips he collected streamed through his mind like data spitting from a computer: ask questions, get her talking about herself; don't talk about your mother; don't talk about religion; stay away from politics; don't be complicated, or eager, or needy; talk about goals, women like men with goals; always look her in the eye, and whenever possible, lean forward to create intimacy.

Ronald leaned forward, jostling his coffee.

"I'm a computer software engineer, product efficiency, that's my specialty. Actually, I'm a consultant. I mean, I run a consulting service that specializes in computer software product efficiency. Computer Software Product Efficiency Consulting, that's the name of my business. It's good. Consulting, I mean. I just finished a project that was good. So it's pretty good." He leaned back into the chair, gathered himself. "But I hate talking about work. I would rather talk about my goals. I mean, the goals I am trying to reach."

Alice smiled demurely. She was wearing a black turtleneck that accentuated long, taut breasts. Her hair was blonde and fine and extended to her shoulders. Her eyes were blue and oval, and her eyelashes ticked at the fragile skin around her cheekbones. She had a long nose that spread at the nostrils, giving off an athletic aura.

"Tell me one."

Ronald blushed. "Dating, I imagine. Meeting someone I like." Worried he sounded too eager or needy, he quickly asked Alice about her goals.

"Me," she laughed. "I'm always working toward a goal. Like right now, I'm training to run in the New York City Marathon. Twenty-six miles. I've never done it."

She paused. "Do you run?"

Ronald looked down at his hands. He was not very athletic, and while thin, hardly exercised. "I run all the time," he lied.

"Have you ever done a marathon?" she asked

"A marathon? No, I mean, not yet. It's a goal of mine. A major goal."

Alice picked up a napkin and wiped at the corners of her mouth. "You can train with me, if you'd like. I run three times a week, five miles, after work, in Central Park. I start at six and end at seven. I'm getting faster. When I started I finished at 7:10. Want to meet me for a run next week?"

"Sure," he said.

"Monday good for you?"

Ronald knew it wasn't. "It's great," he said. "I can't wait."

When Ronald got to the park it was blustery, and the sharp late-January wind burned his newly shaven face. It was early evening and still light, but very cold, and his breath rose in clouds as he strode toward their meeting place at the park's west side entrance. Alice was there before him, stretching her right leg atop a gray metal bike rack. A few feet away on the street were a string of horse carriages, their drivers in top hats and capes encouraging passing tourists to take a romantic spin through the park. The air smelled of horse manure and hot dogs.

"Hey, right on time," Alice said. She was wearing a baggy blue sweat suit and a black, bullet-shaped cotton hat pulled over her ears. "Just let me finish stretching and we'll get going."

Ronald rubbed his shirtsleeves. He was decked out in a one-piece Lycra running suit, black with blue racing stripes that hugged his body like sealskin. He had purchased it the night before. The salesclerk at Speedo had given the gear a strong recommendation, telling Ronald it was "aerodynamic" and would "cut precious seconds from his best time." The pitch was hard to resist, considering Ronald made a living streamlining operations, lightening workloads, reducing complex and time-consuming work to one touch of the computer keyboard. In addition to the suit, he'd also bought a pair of Nikes, silver tipped, and a black wristwatch, its face the size of a baseball, that tallied the miles, yards, feet, even inches he ran at any given time.

Ronald thought he looked like a robot—especially standing next to Alice in her loose-fitting outfit, her body hidden somewhere inside the folds of soft cotton. He was sure the tight suit exposed every bump and knob and dimple on his body. He didn't dare think what an erection would reveal.

Alice finished her stretching and walked toward him.

"Should we warm up with some light jogging and sprints before the long run?"

"Sure."

"How far have you been running lately?" she asked.

"Uh, about a mile or two," he bluffed.

Alice pointed a finger at his sneakers. "New?"

Ronald blushed. "Uh, yeah, my old ones wore out. So I figure now's a good time to buy a pair."

"Do you like them?"

"Yeah, they feel good." He hopped a few times and then looked down and wiggled his toes inside. "Real good."

"I have to admit, I don't wear Nike. You know, the whole slave labour thing."

Ronald didn't follow. This is what worried him: his inability to make small talk. Although he read the paper daily, watched the news, his engineer-trained mind seemed unable to absorb interesting tidbits of pop culture or current events. He could disassemble a computer and return it whole, piece by piece, in an hour. But if you asked him who was in what movie or on what television show he was a blank slate. Of all the things that terrified him after his divorce, the thought of not being able to keep up in conversation with a woman nearly made him retch.

"I shouldn't talk," Alice continued. "I mean, look at me, I don't eat meat but I own a black leather coat. But Nike, you have to admit, is bad."

Ronald swallowed and then coughed into his hand.

"I once volunteered to develop a software system for a conservation organization."

"That's pretty cool," Alice said. "Ready to go?"

Ronald took in a breath. "Sure," he said. "I'm ready."

"You run well."

Ronald grunted into Alice's compliment. He was barely keeping pace with her as they darted through the park, on a thin cement trail dotted with wet yellow leaves and new frost. The Lycra suit was binding, and he was having trouble breathing. The one positive was that he didn't have to worry about getting an erection, as the flow of blood below his waist seemed to have halted.

Alice was an easy runner, with long loping strides that contradicted her diminutive stature. She barely came up to Ronald's armpit and, with her baggy outfit, looked more like his daughter than his date. But her body was well proportioned, and she moved with grace and balance as she dodged oncoming bikers, pedestrians, and other runners.

"We're almost at 5K," she belted out. "We can stop or go an extra mile; push it, if you'd like."

Panic enveloped Ronald. It felt as if someone was jabbing the entire right side of his body with a penknife, and the soles of his feet throbbed. He didn't know the right answer. Stop and Alice might think him weak and not goal oriented. Keep going and he risked vomiting or losing a bowel movement in the smothering suit. He decided to risk defecation. "Let's do it," he spat out. "I feel great."

"Awesome." Alice sped forward, the rapid movement of her feet making him dizzy. "We'll kick it up a notch."

Ronald gulped air and expanded his chest against the gripping fabric. He had never pushed his body to this extreme. His mind, however, had endurance. It was the secret of his work success. He could focus for hours on the most complex problems. He wore them out.

Trailing Alice by several yards, Ronald willed himself to blot out the searing pain, the numbing fatigue wracking his legs, and analyze his movements. "Reduce wasted motion, increase speed," he muttered until the mantra clanged in his brain with each step. Like a suspension bridge locking into place, a new running style took form: his choppy, unbalanced strides became smooth and sure; his flailing arms drew close to his body and pumped in unison; his wobbling head grew ramrod straight and pointed forward, leading his body like the bow of a clipper ship through a clear ocean. Ronald felt a surge of exhilaration as he sped ahead. The cold air whistling past his ears grew louder and louder, but he did not feel the breeze. A near animal energy filled his legs. He was flying.

"Hey," Alice shouted. "Hey."

Ronald was a good 500 feet past her when he realized she had stopped running. He jogged back, embarrassed but elated.

"Wow," Alice panted, pulling her hair back behind her ears. Sweat dripped from her nose and chin. "You were really cooking."

Ronald looked down at his sneakers. They were covered in mud.

"I guess I caught my second wind."

"I thought you were ditching me. Maybe I'm too slow for you to train with."

"Not at all. You're a great runner. I was just doing some extra work, you know, for my marathon goal."

The wind was whipping now, and it was getting dark.

"Do you want to jog back to my apartment and get some water?" Alice asked. "I don't live too far."

Ronald's face was red and raw from the cold and the exertion. He nodded as a drop of sweat rolled off his nose.

"That would be nice," he said. "But can we walk?"

Ronald woke from a dream gasping for air. His running suit and sneakers were thrown in sections across Alice's bedroom's hardwood floor. They had sex almost immediately after entering the apartment. With glass of water in hand, she guided Ronald to her bed, unpeeled the layer of Lycra, and took him. He came quickly. Too fast, he worried, but Alice didn't seem to mind and they wrapped around each other and fell asleep.

In the dream, Ronald was riding a horse through a scorched yellow desert. He was hot and thirsty and covered in a fine dust that choked him. He came upon a white marbled well and dismounted the horse. As he was looking for a hitching post or tree to tie the reins on, a great wind burst upon him and sandblasted his face. But it didn't hurt. It was soft and cooling and melted on his skin like first snow.

When the wind stopped, he was standing alone: the horse was gone and the well replaced by a single green cactus that towered over his head and shielded the sun. He walked to the cactus and gently placed an open palm against one of its pencil-long thorns. He felt no pain and kept pushing until the thorn pierced his skin. When he tried to pull away, the thorn became more deeply embedded in his palm until it penetrated the other side. As he struggled to free himself, another storm hit, more violent than the first, hurling pebbles and sticks and debris across his body.

Ronald's heavy breathing had woken Alice.

"Are you alright?" she asked. Her hair was matted to her head, and her face was whiter and smaller than he remembered. The warmth of her skin under the blankets radiated across his naked body.

"Uh, yeah, sorry, weird dream," he said.

"I love dreams. I'm actually good at analyzing them. Tell me about it?"

"It was just weird."

"Yes, you said that." Alice sat up and crossed her arms. "Why was it weird?"

"I don't know. I mean, I was in a desert, on a horse, riding alone, and I was really thirsty. And a storm came and whipped by me, but the sand didn't sting my face, it was kind of nice and soft. And there was this cactus and I couldn't free my hand from one of its thorns. And another storm came and I woke up. Weird, right?"

Alice leaned forward. Her breasts hung loose. Ronald noticed the left one curved slightly to the right. He felt his erection grow under the sheet.

"Not so weird," she said. "First, you're thirsty in the dream because you're probably thirsty in real life. We ran a lot. You're probably dehydrated. I get those dreams all the time. I'm drinking like gallons of water. Or trying to get water."

"I never thought of that," Ronald said.

"Oh yeah," Alice continued. "Most dreams relate directly to physical needs. Like wet dreams. You ever have those?"

"Maybe, I mean, not lately. When I was a kid."

"Don't be embarrassed. They're natural. It's your body's way of getting rid of what it doesn't need. Anyway, the desert probably represents a journey you are taking. The wind and the storm and the thorn are the dangers and pitfalls you are encountering on the way. It reminds me of a Clint Eastwood movie. One of those westerns he did when he was young. *High Plains Drifter*, I think that's the name. You know, he comes riding into town from the desert on a horse. He's covered in dust and very mysterious. There's something in his eyes that tells you he's been through a lot. Like he knows everything about life."

"That was a good movie," Ronald said. "Very weird."

"Not weird," Alice corrected. "Deep." She reached over and danced her fingers across his midsection. "Maybe you're my High Plains Drifter?" she whispered.

Ronald watched her hands move lower. He exhaled and then leaned over and kissed her lips. He moved atop her body in slow sections: first his shoulders, then his chest, then his stomach and waist, and finally his legs. He waited a few seconds, admiring the contrasting whites of their skin pressed together, before entering her. He thrust in compact, clean strokes, steady and rhythmic and increasing in speed. As he neared climax, he opened the palm of his right hand and held it out in front of his face. He peered into its centre, looking for a thorn, but it was clean and clear and he wondered when it had let him go.

JOSEPH

THAT SUMMER, I had sex on twenty-five different boats, for twenty-five consecutive nights, with one woman: my ex-wife. The goal was to get Madeline pregnant, and although we began with the hope of getting back together after a trial separation, we ultimately ended up further apart and divorced.

The boats Madeline and I commandeered for our trysts were moored at a local marina. We'd wait until well past midnight, after the lone security guard at the gate had departed, before making our way onto the docks. Most nights it'd be eerily quiet once we boarded a vessel, and other than Madeline's measured exhales and my occasional grunts, the only noises we'd hear were the sudden splashes of baby blue fish as they chomped their way through the oil-coated harbour water, shredding with their razor teeth schools of fleeing minnows, chubs, and shiners.

But our final break didn't mean we weren't successful in making a baby; we did conceive a child during that last time together. It must have happened near the end of our sexual marathon, when Madeline was ovulating and we were sticking exclusively to small crafts. Like the eight-foot wooden skiff we wedged into one night that nearly capsized during our lovemaking. The owner had christened the dinghy, JOSIE, spray-painting the name in hot pink across its narrow bow. Of all the boats that summer, it's the only one I remembered in any detail, perhaps because it came close to my own name, Joseph. And when Madeline, to my surprise, offered me the chance to name our daughter after her birth, I decided on Josie, thinking, at least, that a part of me would always be with her.

Madeline and I were both eighteen when we met. She was new in town, and recently hired at a local deli. It was early summer, a Tuesday morning, when I shuffled bleary-eyed into the store for breakfast. At the time, I'd just graduated high school, had no college plans, and was working for tips as a mate on a rusted tub called the *Ole-Lena*. The boat was owned and operated by a Norwegian couple, Ole and Lena Jensen, who charged customers twenty bucks for a half-day of fishing. Work on the Ole-Lena was long, monotonous, and tiring. I had to be on the boat—cutting bait, fixing lines, and preparing rigs—by six a.m. And off it no earlier than six that evening, not allowed to leave until I'd hosed down the decks and mopped up all the fish guts and occasional vomit that had crusted itself to the boat during the day.

The only good part of the job was the fishing itself, when I'd work myself into a frenetic rhythm, flitting like an angry bee from rod to rod, netting and unhooking porgies, fluke, stripers, or whatever was coming over the rails that day. And on days when the bite was really on, when everyone caught their limit, the tips weren't bad either, even though most of the customers were unemployed, middle-aged guys going to seed. These men mostly kept to themselves while fishing, taking quick drags from concealed flasks and smoking cigarettes down to the nub without seeming to inhale. Sometimes I'd see them in town, looking even shabbier on dry land. I always went out of the way to avoid making eye contact, figuring they'd be embarrassed to be seen by someone who knew what they did with themselves each day.

But, looking back, I guess I was the one who was embarrassed. Although I'd pretty much resigned myself even at that early age to a life of manual labour, I wanted to do more than muck out a worn-down fishing boat. My real goal was to scrape enough money together to buy a riding lawnmower and a truck big enough to haul it, then set out a shingle as a professional landscaper. Growing up, it was my job to cut the half-acre of grass surrounding my family's ranch-style home, a chore I always enjoyed. What I liked most was the methodical order of the task, and the tangible outcome of making clean what was once messy. The wh process calmed me, made me feel safe and insulated, the whirr of the mower's engine drowning out the world around me. In this regard, I understood the desire of the Ole-Lena regulars to be left alone. I also craved isolation. That is, until I fell in love with Madeline.

"We're out of eggs," were the first words she said to me as I walked toward the deli's counter. "The delivery truck's late."

I liked that she gave me information I hadn't asked for. I also liked her hair, which was shoulder-length, frayed at the bangs, and coloured a strawberry-blonde. And her eyes, too, which were almond-shaped and inky black, sparkling behind delicate, upturned lashes. Seeing her made me want to jump the counter and give her a kiss. But instead, I did something that even today I don't understand exactly why I did it: I spat on the floor.

"Come here," Madeline said immediately.

I remember inching forward with head bowed, like a spot bowler focusing on the lane arrows and not the pins.

"Closer."

My groin pressed against the countertop.

"Look at me."

I craned my chin up until our eyes locked. The intensity of her gaze caused a wave of prickly heat to course through my body.

"It's my job to sweep up," she said without anger or interest, as if she was reciting the duties listed in her resume.

"I'm sorry," I managed to stumble out.

"I don't like to sweep up saliva," she said.

"I'm sorry," I said again. And then, a thought occurred to me that I should introduce myself. "I'm Joseph."

Her spit hit the bridge of my nose, splattering my eyes.

"Madeline," she said, smiling, her lips glistening.

That night I lost my virginity on the Ole-Lena, having sex with Madeline atop a huge bait chest that I covered with burlap sacks. I still had on my rubber work boots when I entered her, my pants and underwear pushed down below my knees. Madeline was wearing a yellow sundress, the fabric light as lint, and it floated up and down in the darkness with each of my wild thrusts. She warned me before we started that I needed to "pull out" before I came, and although it was not easy for me to time, I did as she asked, removing my penis at climax and shooting a stream of semen past her head and into a bucket filled with broken fishing reels.

"So you've done this before?" I asked after we had cleaned ourselves up and were walking back to the car.

"You mean have sex? Of course. Why?"

"I just hope, you know, it was good for you. I'm not that experienced."

Her voice changed. It was softer, and no longer patronizing.

"You'll get better," she said. "But you'll need to practise with someone who's really good at it."

"With you?" I asked, hopefully.

"Yes," she answered, closing her eyes and tilting her head back for a kiss. "With me."

A year later, we were married.

Josie had to be the prettiest baby ever. She had Madeline's dark eyes, clear olive skin, and a golden fuzz of curls atop her head that reminded me of those baby chicks you want to pick up in your hands and squeeze. Josie also had a mouth as round as a tulip bud, and rosy lips that couldn't sneer if she knew how. She was pudgy too, her elbows and knees invisible in the folds of fat, and her neck full of rolls that jiggled when she laughed, which was about all the time. She even had perfect ears, with teardrop-shaped lobes that Madeline pierced herself and adorned with two faux diamond studs that sparkled as bright as the real thing.

Madeline received full-custody of Josie in the divorce. I did have regular visitation rights—at Madeline's invitation only—and one scheduled weekend with Josie a month. The entire week before these visits I'd fret about the state of my apartment, getting on hands and knees each night to scrub the bathroom floor, and wearing out the rugs with a vacuum. My biggest fear was that Josie would get sick or hurt on my watch, and that Madeline would cut me off from ever seeing her again. So in addition to my hyper-vigilante cleansing, I also handled Josie as if she were a newly-hatched egg, keeping her in my arms almost all the time we were together.

But still, as hard as I tried to return Josie to Madeline in as good a shape as I got her, there were times I failed. Like once, right before Josie turned two, I thought it might be fun to let her sit on my lap as I cut the grass. Things were going well, and Josie was having a great time banging her little hands atop the steering wheel as I weaved around the lawn. But I must have lost attention because I ploughed over a shallow stump, which locked up the blades and propelled me forward, pressing my two hundred pounds against Josie and the steering wheel. I'll never forget her face at the moment of impact, more startled than frightened, as if she couldn't believe I'd done such a thing to her. Then she began crying, loud, piercing screams that eclipsed the decibel level of the hindered mower. I rushed her to the emergency ward, and the examining doctor told me she had two broken ribs. That was truly a horrible time, seeing Josie in pain, and then to having tell Madeline about it. But Madeline's reaction surprised me. She wasn't furious, just concerned for Josie, and even grateful that the injury wasn't more serious.

It was only years later, when Josie turned fifteen and asked a judge for permission to live with me, that Madeline brought the incident up, telling the court I was an "unfit father," someone who'd almost "killed his baby with a lawnmower." But even at that moment, flushed with embarrassment that our family's discord was open to the public, I didn't hate Madeline. In fact, I loved her, and not a mature love, the kind where you know that love is fleeting from one moment to the next and the only thing to do is ride out the bad times until the good ones arrive again, but an irrational, teenage love, a wild lust, where your head swims and nothing makes sense or matters except being with that other person. And Josie, I think, knew that about me—the unquenchable crush I had for her mother. Which is the real reason, I truly believe, she wanted to move in with me: hoping that with the two of us together under one roof, Madeline, might follow. Because you have to know, right up until the moment she died, not long after the judge denied her request to live with me, Josie's one and only obsession was getting her parents back together. And, to be honest, it was always my hope too.

My family didn't think it was a good idea for us to get married. They thought we were too young, too poor, and too much in love to make it work. "The kind of feeling you have for each other goes away quick," my father told me the morning of my wedding, a small affair held in our backyard. "And when it does, you'll need some real things to keep you together." But he was wrong, at least on my end, as I never felt a decrease in the intensity of my love for Madeline: not in the six years we were married, the seven months we were separated, and the twenty-five nights when we tried to rekindle our relationship and make a baby.

I was the one who thought it would be exciting to have sex on boats, in the same marina where the Ole-Lena was once docked.

Madeline wasn't exactly thrilled with the idea, but she did find it more appealing (and less expensive) than renting out motel rooms. At the time, we'd given up our shared apartment, and had both moved into our respective parent's homes to regroup. Neither place was conducive to romance, and to me, the marina harkened back to an innocent, more hopeful time in our lives.

Anyway, Madeline went for it, even though she was still a bit cold and resistant in the beginning. But after a week or so, I noticed a growing synergy between us, a sense of teamwork that had not been present for many years in the marriage. Little things made me think Madeline was warming to me again. Like she would let me open the car door for her when I picked her up and dropped her off, and when we'd finished having sex, she'd linger next to me, even let me hold her hand, not moving a muscle until I suggested we head home.

But perhaps I put too much weight on these signs, because, ironically, it was right after our night on the JOSIE that we had a fight that set the table for our divorce. What I did was go and surprise her the next morning with some flowers at her part-time job. I'd picked out a bunch of daisies from my mother's garden and wrapped a white ribbon around their stems to match their petals. It was Madeline who came to the office door, and she wasn't smiling. "Why are you here?" she asked with a snap. And when I smirked, shrugged, and pointed my gaze at the flowers, she said, "I'm working."

Well I got mad and anxious all at the same time, and didn't know if I should throw the flowers down and walk away or just walk away with them in my hand. So I did neither, and just stood there, until she snatched the daisies away and slammed the door in my face.

The rest of the day was rough on my nerves, as I thought a lot about Madeline's reaction and how she'd always been mean and impatient with me when I was just trying to be nice. Then I thought about the idea I had a long time ago to start my own landscaping business, and how after we married I wanted to take the money we made from the wedding and go buy a professional riding mower and a used pick-up truck to haul it. And how Madeline had nixed the plan right away, taking our money and spending it on a new car for herself, and then arranging for me to go to work with her father at a local tool and die plant. Thinking about all this, I got into such a rage that I purposely picked her up an hour late that night, and during our sex I didn't once look her in the eye. Of course, my anger made Madeline twice as mad, and she jumped out of the car before I could open her door, and told me that we were now "completely through." When I called later to smooth things out, her mother answered and said Madeline didn't want to talk. And the next night, when I came by to pick her up, hoping she might have changed her mind, her father came out of the house and told me never to come back. So I didn't.

Josie's death was not Madeline's fault, but I like to blame her anyway. Madeline was out with girlfriends partying one night and left Josie and her best friend, a girl named Rebecca, home alone together. The girls drank some wine Madeline had left open in the fridge, and I guess they got a little wild because they decided to go hitchhiking. Anyway, they walked to the highway to catch a ride, and a van driven by an elderly man and his wife veered into where they stood on the roadside with thumbs out, killing them both instantly.

The few years since Josie passed have not been easy. I've quit my job, live off the government dole, and drink too much beer. I've even become a regular patron of a local fishing boat, much like the Ole-Lena, where I can sit undisturbed and suck suds out of a bag, watching the water more than my line.

Still, there's Madeline. I know she's not remarried, know she doesn't have a boyfriend, and know she doesn't ever want to see me again, which, for the first time since I met her, I'm fine with—happy, really, because now I have the chance to focus completely on my hurt, and be sad without any reason not to be. And on warm summer nights, when I'm not too drunk or tired from a day's inactivity, I'll head to the marina, pick a boat and nuzzle in for the night, and then just close my eyes and imagine, for as long as my mind will allow, that I'm actually all alone.

HAROLD

AFTER MY wife and I separated, I spent most evenings wandering the cavernous aisles of a local Sam's Club. Shopping was more than a distraction: it gave me a reason to get up in the morning. I am not ashamed to say I was addicted, sweating anxiously through work until the stroke of five, when I would leave my job as a telephone operator and speed over to Sam's. Once behind a shopping cart the size of a four-wheeler, I would lose myself in a retail frenzy, ruthlessly cutting off elderly women with walkers, lost children crying out for their mothers, groggy men wobbling behind their wives, anyone standing between me and a blue light special.

Sam's was closed on Sundays (Blue Laws), so I used the time to perform inventory, strolling through my one-bedroom ranch with clipboard in hand, taking stock of what I had and what I needed. Lack of space was always a problem: my home's narrow, railroad car design was not conducive to stacking and storing in bulk. But I did my best where I could, replacing bookshelves and cabinets with industrial shelving and hanging hooks from the ceiling. I even drained our backyard pool dry and filled it with canned goods. Still it was not enough. But when I went to purchase a snap-together shed for the front yard to store energy bars, I discovered I was broke. In the blush of buying fever, I had not bothered to keep track of my statements—credit card, checking or savings. All three sources of revenue had dried up, and given my limited pay cheque, I would never again be able to purchase in the quantity I had grown to depend on. Faced with this reality, I fell back into a depression, obsessing about my failed marriage, my bleak future, a life without a shopping cart to steady me. It got so bad that I even began to consider suicide.

And I really might have, if I hadn't met a woman.

It happened while I was driving to work. I was lost in thought, lamenting a depleting supply of Twizzlers, and missed the red light. My aging Saturn slammed into the back of a shiny new Black Jeep Chief Cherokee. After peeling my forehead off the windshield, I saw that a woman was pounding on my car door. She was very pretty, with dark flowing hair, violet eyes shrouded in classy false lashes, and a petite figure encased in a matching violet jump suit. I rolled down the window and smiled.

"Can I help you?"

"You asshole. Get out of the car."

It took me some time to accomplish the task. I finally figured out how to work the door handle and stood up with hand extended in greeting.

"Nice to meet you."

"Get back psycho."

I liked her voice, and her painted lips, which continued the violet palette. When she said "psycho" they puckered in and out like a tropical sea anomie.

She whipped out a cell phone, her fingers a blur as she dialled.

"Yes, police, I need help. My car was smashed from behind. We're near the off ramp on Route 7. Could you send someone right away? The other driver is crazy."

"Harold," I interrupted. "My name is Harold Ram, like the animal."

She ignored me and walked over to examine her truck's back fender. There was a sizable dent to the right of a National Rifle Association bumper sticker. She bent down and traced her finger around the damage.

"Do you like guns?" I asked. "Sam's Club sells firearms and ammunition. We could go together and buy some weapons."

She began to cry, making sucking sounds as she inhaled. Her nose began to run and mucus dripped onto her red high heels. I reached down to pat her on the shoulder, but missed completely and lost my balance. My head bounced twice: first off the bumper, and then the pavement. I stared down at the black tar, watching my blood pool and thinking how to ask the woman on a date. When I finally figured out my move and turned to face her, a new face was facing me. This one was beefy, ruddy and pockmarked. His eyes were shaded by a patrolman's cap. His lips were thin and rigid. He looked worried.

"You okay?"

"I'm running out of liquorice."

The cop nodded sympathetically.

"And I only have 10 rolls of paper towel left."

"That is low," he said. "I always keep a minimum of 50 rolls on hand."

I had a sudden urge to steal his gun and race to Sam's, stage a hold up and fill my car with Bounty. And I really might have, if I hadn't passed out.

I woke up in a hospital bed. My head hurt. I reached my right hand up and probed with the tips of my fingers an egg-size welt over my right eyebrow.

"Nice bump you got there."

It was the pockmarked policeman. He rose from a plastic chair near the door and ambled towards the bed. He had an odd, rolling gait that made me nauseous.

"Good to see you up. I need some information. You weren't carrying a wallet or a license at the scene."

The officer took out a notebook and pen.

"Let's start with your name."

"Harold Ram, like the animal."

"Address."

"Two Harmony Lane."

"Phone number."

I gave it.

"And is your wife home? I can call and tell her you're here."

"I'm not married."

The cop smiled. He had a scar on his upper lip. It contrasted nicely with his pockmarks. He pointed to the gold wedding ring on my finger.

"What's that?"

"A memory. I'm getting divorced."

He stopped writing.

"Two Harmony Drive. That's not far from Sam's Club."

"Yes."

"You ever go?"

I nodded, pain coursing across my forehead from the movement.

"Me too. Every Friday. I shop and then hit Sam's Spuds for a beer. Some nice looking women there."

He closed the notebook and smiled again.

"By the way, I'm divorced. Two years. And I've never been happier."

He left and I went back to sleep. I was in the hospital four days total, and my job gave me two weeks sick leave. A few days after returning home, I received a certified letter from Abigail Andres, the woman I hit. On top of the damage to her fender, she was suing me for physical injuries, trauma, and the inability to perform the duties of a girlfriend. I assumed that meant sex, and I got aroused thinking about her violet eyes and lips.

The only other piece of mail was an unmarked envelope. Inside was a note on personalized stationery. It was from the desk of Officer Tom Kelly.

Dear Harold,

I'm the cop from the hospital. Hope you're feeling better. A blow to the head is tough. A perp once smacked me in the coconut with a bat and I was unconscious for three days. But I got over it. You will too. Give me a call when you're up and about. As I mentioned, I usually go to Sam's Club on Fridays. Maybe we can meet and hang out.

Best,

Officer Tom Kelly

That Friday Sam's Club never looked so good. The sight of aisle upon aisle of items, the perfect order of mass perishables, the wonderful machine of unbridled, unrelenting, unconquerable, capitalistic consumption, filled me with joy and passion. I wanted to hug the barrels of caramelized beer nuts, caress the cauldrons of post-it notes, embrace the battalions of batteries and television remotes and staple guns.

Officer Tom Kelly was waiting for me in the Patio Furniture Pavilion. He was reposed on a chaise lounge. He was out of uniform, but still encased in policeman blue: blue jeans, blue work shirt, blue socks, blue sneakers. His pockmarks gleamed under the store's florescent lighting. He stood and smiled as I approached.

"Glad you came. How you feeling?"

"Better. Thanks for inviting me."

He leaned in and whispered into my ear.

"I got an informant here, a clerk in the merchandizing department. He told me these chaise lounges are going on sale tomorrow—$30 bucks a chair. But if you buy five, you get one free."

I looked around to make sure no one was near.

"Do you know of any other deals?"

"I probably shouldn't tell you this, but I hear that next week there's a shipment of Foo Dog Dragons coming in from China."

"Foo Dog Dragons?"

"Figurines," he whispered. "Hand-made out of Jade. I did a little research. A Foo Dog is a mythical beast that was found guarding the gateway to Buddhist temples. In my line of work, I could easily resell them at a high mark-up to store owners who want to keep burglars away. It's going to be a limited supply, maybe only a hundred or so. I'm thinking to buy the whole lot of them, corner the market, so to speak. I could use a partner to keep down the initial costs. Want to go in on it with me?"

I suddenly remembered I had no money. Panic and shame gripped me. I considered running from the store and killing myself. And I really might have, if I hadn't been blindsided by a shopping cart.

The first thing I noticed after the blow was her violet jump suit.

"Hi, Abigail," I said, wincing slightly as pain shot up from my hip where the cart had connected. "I got your lawsuit. It was nice to hear from you."

"You son of a bitch."

"Harold Ram. Remember, like the animal."

She was about to strike me again when Office Kelly stepped between us.

"Calm down, ma'am," he said, resting his hands on the cart. "I'll waive the assault charge if you just walk away right now."

"You're the cop from the other day," Abigail said, surprised. "What the hell are you doing here? Are you friends with this loony?"

Officer Kelly clicked his tongue.

"Please, ma'am. Calling him names, however deserved, will not solve the problem. I think it best if you just move on and finish your shopping."

"Who can shop now? Seeing this freak again has given me a migraine."

I sprinted away, found the aisle with aspirin, grabbed as many bottles and boxes as I could hold, and raced back to the Patio Pavilion. But they were both gone. There was a note taped to one of the chairs. It was from the Desk of Officer Tom Kelly.

Harold,

Abigail and I went to Sam's Spuds. Please go home.

Best,

Officer Tom Kelly

I headed directly to Sam's Spuds. Officer Kelly looked annoyed when he spotted me. He and Abigail were sitting side-by-side at a small table. He removed his arm from the back of her chair as I approached.

"Harold," he said," I thought I told you to go home."

I ignored him and stacked the aspirin on the table in front of Abigail.

"There's Excedrin, Advil, Bayer, Motrin, and Aleve. If you're cramping, I can get a box of Midol."

"I told you he's a psycho," Abigail said. "You should arrest him."

Officer Kelly smiled benignly.

"Harold, do what I say. Go home and rest. We can meet up another time."

"But I love you."

"Me?" Officer Kelly asked.

I pointed at Abigail.

"I want to marry her. Right here. In Sam's."

Abigail pushed her chair out and lunged at me. But Officer Kelly was fast. He held her back with one hand, pushed me away with the other.

"Harold, I'll say this one more time: go home. If you don't go, I'll treat you like any other perp and take you down."

I winked at Abigail.

"A perp once hit me in the coconut with a bat."

Officer Kelly took Abigail gently by the elbow and stood.

"That's enough. We're going. You're staying. Take care, Harold."

I watched them leave, and then sat down at the table. I opened a bottle of Motrin and swallowed four tablets dry. My thought was to order some tap water and finish the rest. And I really might have, if I hadn't come up with a better idea.

Stealing was easy. After leaving Sam's Spuds, I cased a few aisles before focusing on an isolated bin filled with Silly Putty containers. I shoved two each into my front pants pockets and strolled out. The next night I swiped a handful of Chore Boy Scouring Pads and a box of Ring Dings. The following night I slipped a Nerf football under my shirt and a Slinky toy in my shorts. This went on night after night, for several weeks, except for Fridays, when I stayed home, scared to ply my new illicit trade under the nose of Officer Kelly.

Unfortunately, he came to my door. It was Friday, early in the evening, and I was watching a 1973 rerun of the *Price Is Right*. Bob Barker looked young and healthy and an overweight woman from Des Moines was trying to win a new Ford Pinto by guessing how much a half ton of Rice-A-Roni cost. Atop the television were two Foo Dog Dragons I had pocketed earlier in the week. I had also lifted a tube of ultra-violet acrylic from the Arts and Crafts Section, and used it to paint over one of the Foo Dogs. My romantic thought was to present it to Abigail as a wedding gift, or on our first date, whichever came first.

"Officer Tom Kelly," I stammered, opening the door after he rang the bell.

"Hello, Harold. Can I come in?"

I glanced behind me. Except for the two Foo Dog Dragons, I had stored the rest of the stolen goods in the basement.

"I'm a little busy. Can you come back later?"

He looked over my shoulder.

"I actually can't. I'll only be a few minutes. Surely you can spare me that."

I reluctantly opened the door and let him in.

I led him to a chair facing away from the television set.

"Can I get you a beer?"

"Thanks, but no alcohol tonight. I'm on duty."

He caught my look at his clothes: blue blazer, blue oxford shirt, blue slacks, blue sneakers.

"I'm undercover," he continued. "There's been a rash of thefts recently at Sam's and management asked me to look around. I'm going to hang out at the store on my off hours and see if I can't catch the perp."

"Perp," I repeated.

"Yep, I'll get him. I always do."

I sat down across from him on the couch and smiled.

"Have you seen Abigail lately?" I asked.

Officer Kelly grimaced.

"That's a tougher case," he said. "I might have to go undercover on that one too."

I didn't know what he meant, but continued to smile.

"Anyway," he continued, "I was wondering if you have seen anyone acting suspicious at Sam's recently? Anyone who might be my perp."

My face burned crimson.

"I really haven't been there much lately."

He turned and eyed the Foo Dog Dragons.

"But you have been shopping?"

"Just a little—you know, for essentials."

Officer Kelly slapped his knees, and then stood.

"Well I'm sure I'll break the case soon. I'm going through the purchasing logs. Checking items in stock against what is sold. Tonight I'll be going over the Foo Dog Dragon records. I regret I didn't go ahead with my marketing venture, but money is a little tight right now. Anyway, because of the two-for-one deal, the figurines flew off the shelves before I could raise the capital." He paused. "I imagine I'll see your name on the sale's docket."

"I used cash," I blurted out. "So you won't find a record of my sale."

The scar on Officer Kelly's lips straightened out in sections.

"You still had to fill out an information sheet with the purchase," he said. "It was part of the promotion, don't you remember?"

I looked down at my feet.

"Uh, yeah. That's right. I have been forgetful. My head and all."

"Don't worry, I'll look for your form and make sure you filled it out right."

"Thanks," I said.

"Don't mention it. In fact, why don't you come by later and we can look through the records together. Sound okay?"

"Sure."

"So I'll see you later."

"You bet. I'll be by soon."

And I really might have, if I hadn't fled.

After Officer Kelly left I rushed through the house, grabbing anything I could find and stuffing it into my Saturn, including the two Foo Dog Dragons, which I sat up in the passenger side and secured by seat belt. I drove straight for two days, only stopping to grab a few hours sleep on the side of remote roads or to get gas and go to the bathroom. Finally, I wheeled into a Motel 6 on the outskirts of a small rural town. I was exhausted and needed a shower, a change of clothes, and a real night's sleep.

The motel clerk had Buddy Holly glasses and was as thin as a broom handle. He barely looked up as he talked to me.

"Driver's license."

I opened my wallet and handed him the card.

"How long will you be staying, Mr. Ram?"

"One night."

"How will you be paying?"

"Cash."

"That will be $32."

I handed him two twenties, the last of my money, and he handed me back my change and a key. It was a bland room but clean. I opened my bag and took out my toiletries kit. I saw I had forgotten a toothbrush. I went back down to the front desk.

"Is there a Sam's Club nearby?" I asked the clerk. "I need a toothbrush."

He still didn't look up.

"It's about 30 miles from here, right before you get onto the Interstate. I'm sure you can get what you need at the general store next door. But they close at five."

"What time is it now?"

"Almost five."

I sprinted to the general store. The door was still open and an older man was inside sweeping up. The store consisted entirely of one room. An old fashioned cash register anchored a long cedar counter. There were four aisles bisecting the room. The place smelled like a pine forest.

"Excuse me," I said to the older man, "are you still open?"

He stopped and peered at me as if I was daft.

"If I'm here, we're open. What you need?"

"A toothbrush."

He set the broom against the counter and walked over to aisle three. He pulled out a toothbrush and handed it to me.

"This is the last one I got."

"No others in stock?"

"Only carry one kind. And what's on my shelves is my stock."

I followed him to the cash register.

"That'll be two dollars. I'd appreciate it if you have exact change."

I passed him two singles. He dropped the money into the register and handed me the toothbrush.

"Thanks, come again."

"Can I have a bag?"

He frowned.

"It's small. Just stick it in your pocket."

I thought of Sam's Club, where they doubled and even triple bagged items.

"You don't have a bag?"

"Of course we have bags, but I don't want to waste one on such a little thing." He rested his elbows on the cash register. "But if you have to have it, I'll give you one."

I slipped the toothbrush into my pocket. It felt good there. My hands were free.

"I guess I don't have to have it."

"There you go. Have a good night."

I returned to my hotel room and brushed my teeth. I had brought in with me from the car the two Foo Dog Dragons, and I placed them atop the television. Then I went outside for a walk.

It was a clear night and the stars were beginning to emerge. I walked through the parking lot and into a clearing about a hundred yards from the motel. As I was looking up at the sky, I stumbled and landed face first into a ditch. I rolled over. It was surprisingly comfortable, lying in the ditch. It was only about a foot deep and my body was perfectly parallel to the surface. I closed my eyes and pretended to be a patch of grass. I felt a hum of energy pass through me. After about an hour, I drifted into a deep, dreamless sleep.

I awoke to the clicking of crickets and sparks of fireflies who flitted around me like ballet dancers. Directly above shone the Big Dipper. I hadn't seen it since a kid. I stared at it for a while. Then I traced each star in the constellation with my finger. Then I started sobbing, the tears pouring down my face and disappearing into the dirt below. "It's a giant shopping cart," I choked through the tears, "a beautiful, giant shopping cart."

I slept in the ditch all night and returned to my room in the morning. I took a shower and changed my clothes. I packed everything I had into my suitcase except my new toothbrush and the two figurines. I left the suitcase on the bed with a note: "Whoever finds this suitcase can have it and all the items inside, including keys to my Saturn which is parked outside."

I walked down to the lobby, checked out, and then headed to the general store. The owner was leaning over the counter, reading a newspaper.

"Hello," I said.

"Morning."

"Do you remember me?"

"Sure. You were here last night."

"That's me. Listen, would you consider a trade—something of mine for something of yours?"

"Depends on what you're trading, and what you want."

I pulled out the two Foo Dog Dragons and set them on the counter.

"I'll trade you these for a paper bag."

The storekeeper eyed the figurines.

"What are they?"

"Foo Dog Dragons. They're mythical beasts that keep away burglars."

"I don't have any worry about that."

"They're also hand-made in China out of pure jade."

"Why is one of them purple?"

"That's ultra violet. The woman I love has the same eye colour."

He eyed the figurines a moment.

"Why don't you want them?"

"I guess I don't need them anymore. I don't need anything, really."

"Except a paper bag?"

"Yes. That's all."

The storekeeper shrugged.

"I'll give you a paper bag for free."

"No, it has to be a trade—a mutual transaction where both parties are satisfied."

"Seems like I'm taking advantage of you."

"I might say the same of you."

The storekeeper took one last look at the figurines.

"You know, my wife collects chatzkies like these on the mantel over our fireplace. Maybe I'll put them there tonight and surprise her."

"So we have a deal?"

He reached down below the counter and pulled out a brown paper bag.

"Deal," he said, passing me the bag.

"Thanks."

"Don't mention it."

I walked out of the store and headed to the ditch. When I got to the lowest point, where I could not see over it, I opened the bag and dropped in the toothbrush. Then I lay down, staring up at the sky, waiting for darkness to arrive, and also the stars.

T

THOMAS EYED the server
and shapely, dressed in a
She was also heavily made
ivory-coloured foundatio
There was also a consider
and lashes dripping with r
eyes. Although her makeup
sha's, the illuminating effec

"I could see you on a canvas"
She showed off her brace
"I can't tell you how
to be a living work
makeup. I apply
She bit at h
"Are yo
"No"

"Would you like a cookie to go with that?" she asked, handing Thomas his coffee across the counter. "Free chocolate chips today."

Thomas had a sweet tooth but was trying to shed a paunch developed since his divorce became final several months before.

"Sorry, I can't."

"Diabetic?"

"Just on a diet."

She studied him a moment.

"You're not too heavy."

"Thanks," he returned sarcastically.

"I meant it as a compliment. You're just the right size."

"I guess I could have one."

Her open smile revealed blue-metal braces.

"I'll get them."

When she returned she held out a ceramic platter of cookies. Thomas fumbled to pick one up after spotting a sliver of nipple between the folds of her blouse. He recovered and took a bite.

"Can I ask you something?" she said as he chewed.

"Sure."

She brought her palms up to frame the underside of her chin.

"Do I look like a Renoir painting? My face, that is. I know it's a strange question, but I really want to know what you think."

Thomas knew little about art, and other than hearing Renoir's name before, could not recall ever seeing his work. But perhaps because he spotted her nipple again, he decided to bluff it.

again.

…happy that makes me. My goal each day is
…of art. That's why I put so much time into my
…everything with an artist's brush for authenticity."

…er lower lip.

…an actor?"

…May I ask what you do?"

Thomas hesitated.

"I'm an accountant. Not very exciting, I'm afraid."

"Don't be silly. Jobs don't define people. It's not what we do that
makes us who we are, but how we do it."

She paused.

"I'm really glad you're not an actor."

"Why?"

"Because my brother is looking for people who are not actors to act."

Thomas blinked.

"I'm sorry, you lost me."

"It's kind of a long explanation."

"That's okay. I'm not in a rush."

She smiled again.

"Okay, my brother runs a company that re-enacts scenes from clas-
sic novels. It's like those Civil War buffs who dress up as soldiers and
pretend to fight famous battles. Only in this case its readers pretend-
ing to be characters from books. Anyway, he needs one more person
for his next production. But it can't be an actor: that's his rule. I'm
playing one of the parts. Maybe you can join. Do you like to read?"

Thomas didn't, sticking mostly to the sports page.

"Love to," he lied again.

"Awesome. I'll give you my brother's number."

She handed over a business card coloured the same blue as her
braces. Over the phone number was written:

MARTIN STANTION, NOVEL ADVENTURES

"He goes by Marty," she volunteered.

Thomas realized he didn't know her name.

"I'm Thomas, by the way. And you're …"

"Carolyn."

Thomas took in a breath. He hadn't asked a woman on a date since he met his ex-wife nearly ten years before, but now seemed to be the moment to do so.

"Can I get your number too?" he said. "Maybe we can meet up for a drink?"

She nodded at the card in his hand.

"That's my number as well. I live with my brother."

"Oh."

"So if you call, you might get him … or me. It just depends on luck."

Thomas phoned that evening, hoping to get Carolyn. But it was her brother who answered, barking "Marty" into the receiver after one ring. In short order he told Thomas all about his company and the next adventure.

"So," Marty said when he was done, "what do you think?"

"It sounds interesting," Thomas said.

"It *is* interesting," Marty affirmed. "But it's hard work: rehearsing, studying lines, understanding the character. You can't come to me halfway into the adventure and say you want out. Or you're not sure about the part. You have to be decisive."

Thomas grimaced. "Not being decisive" was a character weakness his ex-wife often tagged him with.

"Are you familiar with *The Sun Also Rises*?" Marty continued.

"I've heard of it."

"That's good enough. The book has everything we need for a novel adventure—sex, violence, betrayal. Definitely Hemingway's best. Most will argue for *The Old Man and the Sea*. But a tiny boat in the middle of the ocean is too limiting for my work."

"You said you're going to Spain?"

"Pamplona. We'll be there a week."

"It sounds expensive."

"It's cheaper than if you go on your own. I get a huge discount on airfare and hotels. Anyway, we can go over money later. Are you interested?"

Thomas hesitated.

"How many other actors are there?"

"Six people for six roles: Robert Cohn, Brett, Jake, Bill, Michael, and the matador, Pedro Romero."

"That's a big group."

"We had twice that many for Joyce's *Dubliners*."

"And who would I play?"

"Cohn. Just talking to you over the phone I can tell you'd be great for it. I'm not sure if Carolyn told you, but we don't want actors. Just real people who want to become different people. So what do you say? Are you in or are you out?"

Thomas started to feel pressed. The whole thing sounded very complicated.

"I know you want me to be decisive, but …"

"Thomas," Marty interrupted, "Carolyn is part of the group."

"Yes, she told me."

"Did she tell you she's playing Brett?"

"No."

"Brett has sex with Cohn, you know. At least in the novel."

"I see."

"Last time," Marty said. "In or out?"

An image of Carolyn's nipple popped into Thomas's mind. Things started to seem less complicated. He closed his eyes and visualized the two of them together. And then he gave his answer.

Thomas hadn't expected it to storm when he left the house and hadn't brought an umbrella. But by the time he rounded the block and spotted the café, there was a torrential downpour. He sprinted down the street, making sure to tuck under his shirt the script Stanton had sent to him, along with a contract spelling out the terms of his participation in the adventure. Other than standard legalese about waiving the right to sue in case of injury or accident, one condition—a non-fraternization clause—stood out. It stated that once rehearsals began, and until the end of the adventure, troupe members were not allowed to interact socially or engage in any extracurricular activities without the prior knowledge and approval of Martin Stanton. If the terms of the contract were breached, Stanton had the right to expel the violator from the adventure and keep the fee they paid for joining.

Carolyn unbolted and opened the door for him.

"Sorry it's locked," she said. "But even a *we're closed* sign won't stop customers from coming in. I don't think people read anymore."

Thomas frowned at the puddle gathering around his loafers.

"I'm making a mess."

"Don't worry," Carolyn said. "I have to mop up later anyway."

Thomas glanced across the room where a squat, nattily dressed man stood—an unlit cigarette dangling from his right hand—talking to several other men whom were seated.

"Is that your brother?"

Carolyn looked over her shoulder.

"Yep," she said flatly.

"I hope I'm not late."

"You're fine." She turned back, and with more enthusiasm asked, "Do you like my outfit?"

She was wearing red sweatpants with a matching halter-top and baseball cap.

"Very much."

"Then you'll love these." She peeled back her lips to reveal red-tinted braces. "I got them this morning. I think red mirrors Brett's raw sexuality. She's quite insatiable, don't you think?"

Thomas flushed.

"I guess so."

"Do you think you can stay and help me mop up after everyone's left? I want a chance to go over some things privately with you about our characters."

An erection began to push against Thomas's jeans.

"Isn't that against contract rules?" he managed to answer.

Carolyn lowered her voice to a whisper.

"The contract says we're not supposed to socialize. It doesn't say anything about rehearsing. Brett and Cohn hook up. So if we have sex, we're not being sociable, we're just practising our parts. But it's up to you. If you don't think being inside of me will help you better understand your character, then we won't do it."

Thomas's penis began to throb.

"No," he said. "I need to do it … I mean, I need to understand."

Carolyn smiled.

"Of course you do," she said, taking his hand and leading him toward the others. "We all do."

Pedro Romero—the matador in *The Sun Also Rises* who beds Brett, causing her fiancé Michael and her ex-lover Cohn to spin into a frenzy of drunken violence—was being played by Hector Salas, a mail sorter for the post office. Salas was a foot shorter than Carolyn and so overweight he perspired profusely, even with the air-conditioning cranking. Still, Thomas thought he was the best actor in the troupe.

He held no such regard for the man playing Michael. Quinn was an immense man with an aggressively-genial face that Thomas found repugnant. A welder by trade, Quinn had hands the size of shovels and sausage-thick fingers, which he liked to drum against a tin cup fastened to his belt buckle. It bothered Thomas that Quinn asked Carolyn to fill the cup with coffee several times during each rehearsal, and more so that she complied.

As rehearsals progressed, Thomas found himself more and more suspicious of Quinn and Carolyn. Or perhaps it was Michael and Brett? He was having difficulty differentiating between what was real and what was acting. Much of this had to do with the improvement in the troupe's cohesiveness, including a better retention of their lines, which caused a marked increase in the fluidity of the dialogue. But still, as they were amateurs, there were constant struggles with timing and positioning that required Marty to cut scenes short and make corrections. Sometimes, if an actor repeatedly made errors, he would launch into screaming rages.

Even the ponderous Quinn, who could have easily squashed Marty with a twitch of his forearm, came under attack. It was during a scene where Michael was to denigrate Brett for her dalliance with Romero, but instead of looking upset, Quinn appeared joyful.

"You're enraged with Brett," Marty seethed, stopping the scene. "She's making a fool of you. How can you smile?"

The scene was restarted, but this time it was Carolyn who could not stop grinning.

"Why are you happy?" Marty exploded again. "He's yelling at you."

"It's my fault," Quinn said, shaking his head.

"How is it your fault?"

"Just something silly I said earlier."

"That's why I don't want anyone being friendly with each other. You become close, you have fun, and when you have to be mean in a scene you can't do it. No more socializing, no more favours, and no more …"

"Shut up," Carolyn snapped. "You're the last one to be talking about favours. How many cookies have you sneaked into Salas's knapsack?"

"I'm entitled," Marty returned. "It's important for me to connect with my actors, personally, so I can help them become someone else."

Carolyn locked eyes with her brother.

"Renoir painted only what he saw, not what was there."

"I'm sick of your Renoir fascination. We're not doing Impressionism here. We're not being abstract. We're being real. You'd see this if you weren't so busy …"

"I said shut up."

Marty's face darkened. He pulled out a pack of cigarettes, shook one out, and popped it into his mouth.

"Five-minute break," he grumbled, heading toward the café's entrance.

Thomas stepped toward Carolyn, but she brushed past him on her way to Quinn. "Are you okay?" she said, placing her hand atop his.

"I'm fine," Quinn said.

"Are you sure? Is there anything I can do?"

A smile spread across his large lips. He nodded toward his belt buckle.

Carolyn unhooked the cup.

"Whole milk, no sugar?"

"You know how I like it."

Thomas waited until Carolyn had gone behind the counter. Then he headed to the bathroom, shut the door behind him, knelt in front of the toilet bowl, and vomited—retching until all that came up was bile and blood the same shade as Carolyn's braces.

Thomas and Carolyn continued to have sex right up until the final rehearsal. Although his desire for her remained strong, there was an emotional divide between them that seemed to grow wider with each passing week. It was simple to blame the non-fraternization rules for the chasm. But this was not the only issue impeding a deeper relationship. Even in the private confines of the back counter, Carolyn repelled any physical interaction—foreplay or after-snuggling—ancillary to the act of intercourse. She would merely pull down her bell-bottoms (she never wore panties), spread her legs, and wait for him to roll on a condom and enter her.

Despite this coldness, Thomas was certain he loved Carolyn. And although he was not sure she felt the same, he hoped one day she might. What he envisioned, once the adventure ended, was a series of traditional dating activities: movies, dinners, long walks, candy and flowers, and sappy love notes. He saw these times ending in a simple kiss or embrace, as if to introduce innocence and a normal courtship order to a relationship begun with sex. Their lovemaking would also be different. No longer would it be two orgasms and a handshake good-bye. Instead, they would fall asleep in each other's arms, awaking in the morning with a peck on the nose, a squeeze of the shoulder, and talk, lots of talk, about their past and their present and their future.

It was at the end of the last rehearsal that Thomas learnt Quinn was also recently divorced. Carolyn had gone in the back room and emerged with a bottle of champagne to commemorate the occasion. Quinn had done the honours of uncorking the bubbly and pouring it out for everyone in espresso cups.

"I want to thank you all for coming into my life," Quinn said, pushing in front of Marty. "I was really down after my divorce came through. But this"—his voice cracked—"brought me back to life." He brought the cup to his lips. "Cheers."

Thomas hated to admit that Quinn's words moved him, that he felt empathy for his pain. But this feeling vapourized after Carolyn, champagne residue on her lips, sidled up and whispered to him, "Not tonight."

Thomas's stomach knotted.

"But it's our last time before Spain."

"I'm sorry. I have other plans."

The next moments were foggy. Thomas's eyes glazed, his hearing shut down, and a thin film of cool sweat enveloped his body. He knew enough about panic to know he wasn't dying, but still he worried he might faint or run screaming around the room. But Quinn unintentionally helped Thomas regain some focus by herding everyone (except Carolyn) out of the café.

The logical thing for Thomas was to walk straight home, but he wasn't feeling logical. He pretended to walk away but then doubled back and took sentry in a playground across the street, hiding behind a jungle gym. He watched with despair, sure that Quinn would return to the café to meet Carolyn. But the light inside went off, and Carolyn emerged. Thomas watched her lock the door, drop the key into her tote bag, and stride down the street. He exhaled with relief, figuring she was going home alone.

"Hey, Cohn."

Thomas had dusted himself off and was crossing the street when he turned and saw Quinn coming toward him.

"Why are you still here?"

"I forgot something in the café."

Quinn stepped closer. Thomas smelled the combination of coffee and champagne on his breath.

"What did you forget in the café?"

Thomas thought fast.

"My hat."

"You're lying. You don't wear a hat. Brett wears a hat, a lovely red one," Quinn said, dipping into the Scottish accent he used for his character.

"No, really, I left my hat."

"Okay, if that's what you want to call it."

Thomas tried to decipher meaning from Quinn's words.

"Anyway, glad I ran into you. Let's go get a drink."

Before Thomas could answer, Quinn grabbed his right shoulder and spun him around so they were both pointed toward a neon-lit cocktail lounge at the block's end.

Thomas pulled away from his grip.

"No thanks."

Quinn pulled out a leather wallet bulging with bills.

"My treat."

"Sorry," Thomas said. "But no."

Quinn's eyes stopped their sloshing. His lips were rigid as he spoke.

"You're just like Cohn. No fun. No wonder Carolyn doesn't want you anymore."

Thomas's face reddened.

"How do you know?"

"Didn't you hear her tonight?"

"Yes, but I didn't think anyone else did."

"Of course we did. She said it in front of everybody: 'I'm so sick of him. He depresses me so.'"

"You mean, Brett. That's what she said to Cohn."

Quinn ignored the statement.

"Can't say she said anything nice about me either," he said. "We're both goners now she's found someone new to screw."

"Carolyn or Brett?" Thomas asked. "You're confusing me. Which one is screwing someone new?"

Quinn looked at Thomas as if he was daft.

"They're one person, you know."

"I mean, who is the new guy she's screwing?"

Quinn laughed derisively.

"You really are like Cohn. Desperate as the day is long."

"Just tell me who."

"If I do, will you have a drink with me?"

"Yes."

"Promise?"

"I promise."

"Okay." Quinn said. "But first let's have the drink."

Quinn started crying halfway through his whisky sour. Thomas was nursing a sloe gin fizz that tasted like skunked Kool-Aid. It was "salsa night" at the bar, but other than the two of them, the only other patrons were three middle-aged men drinking in relative silence at the felt-edged bar. The lone woman was the bartender. She was chubby in denim coveralls. A blue sequined cowboy hat shadowed her eyes. She had spotted them drinks on the house, which Quinn, when they had taken a seat at a table near the entrance, told Thomas was because he was a big tipper.

"That's what I always do," he said, taking a pull from his glass. "I lay down a sawbuck before I open my mouth. That generates gratitude."

He waved at the bartender, who tipped the brim of her hat in acknowledgement.

"I think she wants to screw me, but she looks too much like my ex."

Quinn took in more of his drink. When he set it back down, Thomas saw that he was crying, silent tears which fell into his whisky sour.

"I'm a mess," he said.

"I thought you felt better, right? That's what you said at rehearsal."

Quinn lifted his glass, picked up the napkin, and used it to dry his eyes.

"It feels good to break down," he said, tossing the napkin to the floor. "It's not manly to say so, but crying is better than sex."

The bartender brought over another round. She placed them over fresh napkins.

"Just put it on my tab," he told her. "I'll square up later."

"Promise," she winked.

"You know it."

"See," Quinn said after she left. "She wants to screw me."

Thomas pushed his new sloe gin fizz next to the other, which was still nearly full.

"My ex cheated on me," Quinn continued. "She was screwing a co-worker."

Thomas took a sip from his first drink. It didn't taste as bad as before. He took another swallow and then gulped down the rest.

Quinn suddenly slammed his fist on the table.

"You know what I think," he fumed. "I think American women don't get American men. That's why I'm only going to be with foreign babes from now on. Once this adventure's over I'm going to tour Europe. I'm going to travel, drink whisky sours, and screw anything not from here."

Thomas was beginning to feel the effects of the gin.

"I thought you liked Carolyn?" he said.

"I'm a good actor," he said. "I didn't know that until this adventure. But I can fake feelings."

"So you don't like Carolyn?"

"I told you I'm into foreign babes. I like Brett. Her British accent turns me on. The only problem is she doesn't talk when I screw her."

Thomas's lips went numb.

"You're screwing Carolyn?"

"You don't listen," Quinn said. "I'm screwing *Brett* … Michael, I mean. He is screwing Brett."

Thomas finished the second drink in sloppy slurps.

"So who's this new guy?" he asked bitterly. "Romero?"

"No way in hell." Quinn laughed.

"What about Jake?"

"Are you blind? He and Romero are getting it on with each other. Just like Cohn: so focused on a woman you don't see anything else."

"Just tell me who he is."

"Nope"

"You promised."

Quinn sneered.

"I lied."

"That's not fair."

"It's for your own good … all of ours. If I tell you who she's screwing you'll go crazy like Cohn did in Pamplona and ruin the whole adventure." Quinn glanced over at the bartender. "And I really need to get to Spain and start screwing some foreigners. Trust me, the thing to do is forget all about it and get drunk."

Thomas was not a good drunk. Alcohol made him stubborn, it made him clumsy, but mostly it made him sick. He'd staggered away from the table after chugging his fourth sloe gin fizz, weaved his way to the bathroom, and vomited into a urinal.

When he came back out Quinn was at the bar.

"Come here, Cohn," he said. "Let's do some shots."

Thomas lurched forward.

"I'm not Cohn."

"Okay, you're not Cohn."

Thomas tried to focus on the bartender. She'd removed her cowboy hat, and he saw that she wore her brown hair closely cropped, almost a crew cut.

"I'm not Cohn," he told her.

"Yeah, you told us already," Quinn said. "Why don't you go sit back at the table, and I'll call you a cab."

"I don't want a cab. I want Carolyn."

Quinn put a hand on Thomas's shoulder, turned him around, and guided him toward the table.

"You need to go home and sleep it off."

"I need to sleep with Carolyn."

Thomas tried to pull free, but Quinn tightened his grip.

"Let go of me."

"I'm going to get you a cab."

Thomas whirled and took a swing at Quinn. The punch was quick and powerful and on target. He watched his right hand crash into Quinn's jaw as if in slow motion. More surprising was his second punch, a left hook. It connected with Quinn's right ear, sent him toppling sideways, and the big man landed, face first, on the floor.

The bartender was on Thomas in a second. She pointed an aluminium baseball bat at his torso.

"Beat it, Cohn," she threatened. "Or I'll call the cops."

"I'm not Cohn."

"I don't care," she said. "Get out."

Thomas peered at Marty's business card. He ticked off the building numbers as he walked until he came to the address on the card. He slipped the card back into his pants pocket. The run had sobered him. He no longer felt drunk, just disconnected from inhibition. He didn't know exactly what he was going to say or what he was he going to do if he found Carolyn and another man together, but he'd made up his mind to say something and do something.

That's what he admired about Cohn in *The Sun Also Rises*. Cohn wasn't like Michael. Wasn't like Jake. He wasn't a passive victim of Brett's cruelty. He was a fighter. Cohn let it all hang out in Spain:

knocking down all of Brett's lovers—Michael, Jake, Romero—in a jealous rampage. Even though Cohn had crawled his way out of the novel in tears, a beaten, shamed, pathetic character, Thomas saw him as a winner, saw in Cohn how he should have reacted when his ex-wife told him of her affair. If Cohn had been in his place, he would have destroyed the other man. But Thomas had done nothing, just watched her pack in silence, and then retreated into a life of loneliness.

Until Carolyn, that is.

Thomas climbed the three steps to the front door, grabbed the brass knocker and rapped hard until he heard footsteps.

"Yes."

He recognized Carolyn's voice.

"It's Thomas."

She opened the door a crack, the safety latch on.

"What are you doing here?"

Her face startled him. It was the first time he had seen her without makeup. Her skin was drawn and pockmarked, her eyes closer set together, her nose slightly hooked.

"Where is he?"

"Who?"

"The new guy you're screwing."

The door closed. Thomas heard the latch slide. The door opened.

"Come in."

Thomas stepped into a spacious yet stark room. There were no pictures on the white walls and little furniture. The room opened into an exposed kitchen. A hallway leading to another part of the unit was to his right.

"Where is he?"

Carolyn bit at her lip. She was wearing a red terry cloth robe. The tops of her bare feet looked scaly and dry.

"What if someone is here?" she said. "What are you going to do about it?"

Thomas paused to regain his thoughts.

"You sleep with me, you sleep with Quinn. Now you're sleeping with someone else. Are you Brett or Carolyn?"

"Why does there have to be a difference?" she said. "I told you my goal was to become a living work of art."

"But you're not."

"Wrong," Carolyn snapped back. "I'm a beautiful creation."

Thomas felt a surge of meanness tear through him.

"You're not beautiful," he said. "You're ugly."

"Don't talk to her like that."

Marty burst down the hallway with fists drawn. Thomas ducked a wild right, and countered with his own to the shorter man's stomach. The blow caused Marty to lower his guard and gasp for breath. This allowed Thomas several clean shots to his face.

"Stop it," Carolyn shrieked.

Marty winced, tried to throw a punch at Thomas, and crashed to the floor.

Carolyn passed Thomas, knelt at her brother's side, and cradled his head.

"How can you be so vicious?" she said to Thomas.

"He came at me."

"Don't lie," Carolyn returned. "You want to hurt him."

Mary shook his head, spaying droplets of blood from his nose onto Carolyn.

"Please get up," she whispered. "Get up and let him knock you down again … just like the book."

"But I don't want to get hurt anymore," Marty said.

"Get up," Carolyn snapped. "I want art in my life. Play your part or I will stop sleeping with you."

Thomas dropped his guard.

"I don't understand … how could the two of you … "

Carolyn looked up angrily.

"Don't be silly. He's not my brother."

"You lied to me."

"Not me … Brett."

Thomas felt as if he had been punched.

"You never cared about me. I was like everyone else … part of your adventure."

"*Our* adventure."

Marty rose groggily. He lurched forward and swung blindly at Thomas and missed. His momentum took him back to the ground, where he lay face down.

"That's not how it's supposed to happen," Carolyn raged. "Get up and let Thomas hit you again."

Thomas smiled. He suddenly felt calm, in control.

"I'm not Thomas," he said. "I'm Cohn."

He placed his foot over Marty's head, training his eyes on Carolyn. The final line of Hemingway's novel passed over his lips as if spoken by someone far, far away.

"Isn't it pretty to think so?"

Then he stomped down hard.

HERMAN

HERMAN HAD gout and his doctor recommended hot yoga as a cure. The idea behind the practice was to sweat out toxins while contorting the body into positions that encouraged blood flow. The doctor insisted it had worked miracles for many of his patients. He also mentioned it was a good place to meet new people and make friends. Herman, divorced, lonely, with swollen ankles and pained feet, decided to give it a try.

The lithe young woman wearing a black sports bra and matching bike shorts behind the front desk explained the class in more detail. She introduced herself as Lydia and told Herman she was not an official employee, but "helped out" at the studio in return for free classes. The main goal for beginners, she said with an affirming nod, was to "stay in the room" for the entire class; that the heat was the greatest challenge to overcome, but the benefits were worth the discomfort. She herself attended class three times a week, and credited this diligence with ridding her once "absorbing" sugar and caffeine cravings. She also said that her general mood had improved as well.

Herman had come directly from work to the class and felt stodgy (and uncomfortably warm) in slacks, turtleneck and sport coat as he talked with Lydia. Perhaps sensing his unease, she encouraged him to change and then come back to take care of payment. Herman did as he was told, heading into an adjacent men's locker room where he put on a pair of baggy basketball shorts that hung below his knees and an oversized T-shirt with the sleeves removed. It was his standard workout gear, when he did work out, several years before when he was still married and joined a gym as a device to get out of the house and look at women. But this felt different, not because he was less interested in women, but because his main goal was to get healthy, or at least healthier. The doctor's diagnosis had shaken him—gout was an "old man's disease," or so he always thought. And while he knew he could never recapture youth, he was not ready to resign himself yet to middle age.

Herman returned to the front desk and waited as Lydia spoke with a man of about his age, but considerably thinner, and while equal in height, much longer of leg. Snug under his left arm was a rolled purple yoga mat. When he turned to head to the changing room, the end of the mat nearly clipped Herman's chin. He did not apologize or look back as he went to the locker room.

Lydia smiled woodenly as Herman stepped up.

"There you are," she said. "Do you need a mat and towel? We also sell water."

"I need everything."

She reached under the counter and passed him a folded white towel.

"You can grab both over there." She pointed across the foyer, where a mini-refrigerator and a stack of different coloured mats were piled.

"How much do I owe you?"

"Eight dollars for the class, two each for the water and mat, and one for the towel." She wrinkled her nose as she processed the information in her head. "Thirteen."

"My lucky number."

Herman passed over a ten and a five and she returned him two singles. People were now streaming into the studio, all seemingly young, thin and attractive. A flush of insecurity gripped him.

"Should I go in now?"

"You just have to sign this." Lydia passed him a sheet of paper and pen. "It's a waiver excluding the studio of liability should something happen to you during the class."

"What might happen?"

"I'm sure nothing. It's for the lawyers."

"That's what I am."

"So you know about these things?"

"I do."

Herman signed and passed the paper back with the pen. He exhaled nervously.

"I'm worried I won't be able to do it."

"Don't. Carlos, the instructor, is really great. And you're welcome to put your mat next to mine. Sometimes it helps to be near someone who's been doing it a while the first time."

"Thanks," Herman said, blushing lightly.

"No problem. My mat's the aqua one, all the way on the left in the front.

Herman grabbed a water bottle and a mat, and headed into the class. The room was a long rectangle, with a blue-carpeted floor and white-stucco walls. A bank of windows spanned the left side wall, providing a view of another building's grimy backside. He crossed the room and placed his mat next to Lydia's. He saw others in the room spreading towels over their mats, and he did the same. He was about to sit down when the man from the lobby walked toward him.

"You're in my spot."

"Excuse me?"

"That's where I sit."

Herman looked toward the door.

"The woman in front told me to sit next to her. It's my first time."

The man's smile did not lack compassion, but he held it just long enough for Herman to feel as if he was being pitied.

"She must have misspoke. There's plenty of room in the back."

Herman smiled as he moved his mat several feet behind Lydia's, even though he was disappointed with himself for not standing his ground. This willingness to comply with the desires of others, even if they stunted his own, was a longstanding issue, something he knew held him back in the legal profession, which valued the ability to confront and conquer. But despite his best intentions to be more assertive, his natural passivity often overtook him, particularly in moments of stress.

The man watched Herman set up before rolling out his own mat. He sat down facing the mirror, his legs crossed underneath him. From this position, he twisted his torso, leading with his left shoulder, and looked directly at Herman.

"Can I ask you a question?"

"Sure."

"Are you ill?"

"No." Herman said, startled.

"Your feet are swollen."

Herman felt suddenly ashamed.

"I have gout."

"That's what you *have*," the man said matter-of-factly. "It's not your problem. Feet are like canaries in the coal mine—they house the symptoms, not the cause. Trust me, the problem's elsewhere. Most likely you have a blockage somewhere in your body. Your energy, your chi, is getting held up. That's why you're suffering."

He nodded solemnly.

"My name's Charlie. Let's talk after class. I can help you get un-clogged."

Just then Lydia walked in. She glided across the room, weaving gracefully between people and their mats. She smiled at Herman and knelt down on her mat, facing the mirror. The man, Charlie, turned his attention to her.

"Did you think anymore about what I said?"

Lydia spread her arms wide and closed her eyes.

"Well?" he continued.

"I'm starting my practice now," she said calmly, eyes still closed. "You should do the same."

Herman watched as Charlie opened his mouth as if to speak, and then shut it back tight and closed his own eyes.

"Anyone new to the practice?"

It was the instructor, Carlos, who entered the room with a rush and took position in the front of the assembling class. Herman was surprised by his appearance: Carlos was short of stature and pudgy around the waistline, with visible belly rolls under the tight white mesh shirt he was wearing. But his legs were lean and muscular, and his face, accentuated by large, almond-shaped brown eyes and curly black hair, strikingly handsome.

Herman glanced about him. No one had a hand up. He hesitated to lift his, not wanting to draw attention to himself.

"He's new."

It was Charlie. He jerked a thumb over his shoulder.

"Is that true?" Carlos asked.

"I'm afraid so," Herman said.

"It's not a crime," Carlos laughed. "You can't get anywhere in life without starting somewhere. Just do your best. I'm sure you already heard, but the only goal for you today is to stay in the room the entire class. The only rules are to not drink water until after the warm-up series, and then only after each set of poses is completed. Try to concentrate on your image in the mirror. If you want to sit out a pose and see how others are doing it"—he pointed to Lydia—"she's a good one to watch."

Carlos clapped his hands.

"Everyone stand for the first breathing exercise."

He cupped his hands under his chin and spread out his arms like a chicken.

"Begin."

Herman, emulating the others, squeezed his arms together so the elbows touched, leaning back his head in the process and blowing out a whoosh of air toward the ceiling. This motion was repeated ten times.

After the breathing exercise, Herman was sweating profusely. By the end of the warm up phase, he felt on the verge of collapse. Twice he thought he might even vomit. But while Carlos's gentle encouragement was helpful, it was Lydia's example that really kept him going. He watched with fascinated admiration as she moved from pose to pose, the lines of her body flowing beautifully into position, her face a study in concentration. Because he was directly behind her, their reflections in the mirror melded, so that his image was on the outside, while she was the centre. It made him feel as if they were moving together.

Charlie, by contrast, was having a difficult time, falling out of poses, shaking his head and muttering. After one such episode, Carlos, who paced the room while giving instruction, asked people to "accept where their body is at the moment and not get discouraged by its limitations."

The second half of the class, the seated series, was easier for Herman. Most of it was done lying on his back, stretching his legs and lower back. He was still sweating ferociously, but he no longer felt ill or feared he could not finish.

"We started with breathing," Carlos said, after they had completed their last pose. "And we end with it."

He timed their inhales and exhales by clapping his hands, modelling the breath by pushing his diaphragm in and out like a boxer's jabs. When done, he gave a final clap.

"You worked hard, now is the time to reward that work. Rest on your mat and give yourself time to reflect and just be." He paused. "*Namaste.*"

The class repeated the word. Then there was silence.

Herman took in a long breath. He was completely spent, but also exhilarated. For the first time in weeks, he felt no pain in his feet. And he was in love. It was true he found Lydia very attractive, but it was more. He had felt connection with her during the class, a powerful sharing of the soul. He knew it was probably ridiculous and without rationality, but he could not stop the feeling, nor did he want to. It had been some time since he experienced such a strong physical and emotional pull toward a woman. It made him feel, simply, alive.

As he lay on the mat, he mapped out a plan to win over Lydia. Even if she was single and looking, he knew the odds were against him, but he was determined to give it a try. His first idea was to get to know her more by attending class whenever she did—even if it meant him coming, like her, three days a week. This slow-moving yet steady method of courtship had worked with his wife. He first spotted her working at a coffee house, and had spent a full year buying lattes and cinnamon buns before finally asking her out.

Satisfied with the strategy, Herman picked up his towel and mat. He glanced at Lydia, who was lying serenely on her mat. She caught his gaze and smiled. He could not help a smile of his own. He carried it out the door where Carlos was waiting.

"So how did you like it?"

Herman placed his towel in a wicker hamper and laid his mat over a railing.

"I liked it a lot. It was helpful to watch the woman, Lydia, like you said. Do you know which days she comes to class?"

"Of course," Carlos smiled. "Whenever I teach."

"Oh."

"Just check the schedule to see when I'm here," he continued.

"I will."

In the changing room, Charlie stood naked except for a thin towel wrapped around his waist. His lips were set in a scowl.

"You'll need more than this to clear your blockage," he said, reaching into a locker and pulling out a business card, which he handed to Herman. "I do sound healing. It's not a pretty analogy, but I'm like a plumber."

Herman studied the card.

"My website is on there, if you want to learn more."

"Okay."

"So you made it through your first class?"

"I did," Herman said, exhaling. "It's tough, but I feel good."

"You'd feel even better with a good instructor."

"I thought he was fine."

"You haven't been doing it long enough. When you get someone who really pushes, it's amazing."

"Does he, Carlos, I mean … do you know his relationship to the woman who was in front of me?"

"Relationship? He's her instructor."

Herman kept his eyes on the card.

"I guess I'm asking if she's single?"

"I hope so. She just got divorced."

Charlie's eyes hardened.

"You're thinking of asking her out?"

"I'm probably too old for her."

"I wasn't," Charlie said flatly.

"I don't understand."

"I'm her ex-husband."

"Oh."

"I would stay away from her if I were you," Charlie said, his gaze centreing on Herman's chest. "She's blocked too, but won't let me help her. You can't have a good life with someone like that."

Charlie headed to the shower. Herman was anxious to leave and towelled off fast and threw his clothes on. He was still sweating as he passed through the lobby.

"Take care."

It was Lydia. She was back behind the desk.

"Will we see you again?"

"I don't know," Herman said, looking down at the floor. "Maybe it's a little too much for me to take on."

"That's too bad. You were really good today."

"Thanks."

"I hope you change your mind."

Herman nodded. He pushed through the door and went outside.

It was dark and the air was brisk. He pulled up the collar on his coat and walked the few blocks home. Outside his apartment, eyeing the dark windows inside, he realized the ache in his feet had returned. He flipped Charlie's business card into the trash. Perhaps it was time not to do what he was told.

MARTIN

"YES?"

Martin's assistant, Jillian, opened the door to his office just wide enough to stick her head inside.

"Mr. Rigby is outside. He would like to see you."

Martin felt his chest constrict. Rigby was in charge of the company's human resources department. He was somewhat of a recluse, biding his time in a windowless office filled with files and forms. There were rumours he played a larger role than just administrative when it came to personnel decisions. This, and because Rigby's standard mode of communication was by email or paper memo, made the morning's visit unique. But to Martin it was alarming. For the past several quarters the marketing team he headed had not performed up to par, and with sales low he feared Rigby might have been sent to discuss a buyout or some sort of package to grease the wheels for his release.

"Can he come back another time?"

"I'll ask."

Jillian disappeared for a few moments while Martin continued to worry. When she returned she stepped inside and shut the door behind her.

"He says he needs to talk with you this morning," she said, her voice low. "I told him you're very busy. He says he can wait until you're free."

Martin exhaled. If it was bad news, he thought, better to get it over with now than obsess and fret about it all day.

"No, I'll see him," he finally said. "Just give me a moment to get ready."

Jillian glanced at her wristwatch.

"I'll wait five minutes and then send him in."

Jillian left, closing the door once again. He could hear her in the outer office talking to Rigby. He eyed his own wristwatch and then opened the right bottom drawer of his desk. Inside were several bottles of pills. He lifted out one with a yellow label and popped the lid with his thumb. He shook a white tablet into his palm and swallowed it down with only his saliva. It was anti-anxiety medication prescribed by his internist. He had gone in complaining of chest pain, but after a battery of tests the problem was diagnosed as stress.

After returning the bottle, Martin leaned back, closed his eyes, and waited for the medication to kick in. But he felt no more relaxed when he heard Jillian's voice again, followed by a single knock on the door.

Martin righted himself in the chair, doing his best to look calm.

"Come in."

Rigby entered as if not trusting he was welcome, inching his body past the door.

"Jillian told me you can see me now."

"Yes. Sorry to make you wait. I was inundated as usual with sales calls and new revenue opportunities. Please, have a seat."

Rigby chose the far right of two chairs placed in front of the desk. Martin, despite his nervousness, could not help but to admire the sober neatness of the man: from his military style haircut and impeccably shaved face, to his black business suit, white collared shirt, and dark-striped necktie.

"It's been awhile," Rigby said, settling in. "How are you?"

Martin wondered if the question was a trap, a well-meaning ploy by Rigby to get him to voice his insecurities, to open up and expose a weakness that might help the company validate a decision to let him go.

"Me," he said, shooting Rigby his best smile. "I'm absolutely fabulous."

It was not his first lie of the day, but it was the biggest. At the moment, he felt as far from fabulous as any time in his life. In addition to the chest pain and job worries, he was also having problems at home. For one, his ex-wife was petitioning the court to increase his monthly support to their only child, a 16-year-old daughter who was already costing him a fortune in private school tuition. He was also having trouble with his girlfriend, who, at thirty, was fifteen years his junior. Although they had been together only a year, she was pushing for marriage, something he vowed never to do again after his divorce.

They fought regularly about the issue, and when they weren't fighting, she sulked. To cope, in addition to the pills, he was drinking more, supplementing his usual two glasses of wine a night with an equal number of gin and tonics.

"In fact," Martin continued, holding the grin until his lips began to tire. "I couldn't complain if I wanted."

"That's wonderful," Rigby said, bringing his hands together so that the tips of his fingers formed a mini-pyramid. "Unfortunately, my news might dampen your mood."

Martin's heart began to race. He released his smile and glanced at the desk drawer, wishing he had taken an extra pill.

"It's your assistant," Rigby continued. "We have to let her go."

Martin looked up. A wave of relief washed over him. He liked Jillian, valued her skills, but it was better her than him.

"Is this a cost-cutting measure?"

Rigby lowered his hands and leaned forward in the chair.

"Actually," he said, "it's a legal matter."

"She's in trouble with the law?"

"Immigration. She's been working in this country illegally."

"You're kidding?"

"It appears her visa expired years ago."

Martin blinked with confusion.

"Jillian's not a citizen?"

Rigby pressed back in the chair and shook his head.

"Born in Wales. She never told you?"

"Maybe, but I don't remember. We never talk much about personal things. I mean, she doesn't have an accent ... does she?"

"Not a trace."

"So you can see how I wouldn't know. It's not something one asks about, right?"

Rigby shrugged his shoulders.

"I certainly would have told you if I suspected anything," Martin concluded. "You must believe I'm as surprised as anyone by this."

Rigby nodded.

"I imagine it's a shock. Arrangements can be made for you to talk with a counsellor. Someone to help you process any difficult feelings you have about the loss."

"Loss?"

"Jillian was with you for many years. It's normal to be upset."

Martin rubbed the underside of his chin. He did not want Rigby to think him uncaring and callous, but he also did not want word to get out within the company that he needed a counsellor to deal with his feelings. Competent men and women were always after his job, and with sales tanking, someone ambitious might feel emboldened to topple him, if they thought he was vulnerable or losing his grip.

"Thank you for the thought," he finally said. "It's a loss, as you say, but I'll do what I always do in times of strife: put my best foot forward and work that much harder."

"That's a great attitude, Martin. We won't leave you short-handed. We've already started to interview candidates to replace Jillian."

Martin nodded. It made him nervous to think how fast the company moved on things of this nature. Still, he hoped he might be given a say on a new hire. Now that he thought of it, if given the chance, he would prefer another woman, perhaps someone younger than Jillian, a little taller, more slender around the hips ...

Rigby cleared his throat, interrupting Martin's fantasy.

"I'll arrange for Jillian to come to my office before the end of the day. From there she'll be escorted out by security. Sometimes, in these cases, people have a tendency to feel sorry for someone and will let something slip out that makes things messy. So be careful. We want to do everything we can to minimize a scene ... or something worse."

Martin winced, remembering an upsetting moment with his girl-friend the night before. They were at an expensive restaurant, at a prime centre table. He said something she didn't like right after their entrées were served and she threw down her fork, nearly cracking the plate. She stomped out, leaving him with two full meals and the entire restaurant staring at him.

"Don't worry," he said, tapping his lips with a forefinger.

"Good. That's very good."

Martin waited for Rigby to continue, or to get up, but he did not speak or move, just sat focusing on his hands. The silence between them extended long enough that Martin began to feel antsy, his mind drifting to other things he needed to do, including calling his lawyer to see what could be done about his ex-wife's petition.

Ordinarily, he would have politely encouraged Rigby to leave, but with what just happened to Jillian, he felt it best to not make a move and, at least appear, patient.

After Rigby let out a sigh, Martin felt compelled to talk.

"Is everything okay?"

"I'm sorry," Rigby said, looking up. "It's just that something is on my mind lately ... it's personal."

"Personnel ... more firings?"

"No, no, I mean personal ... about me."

"Oh."

"I apologize to even talk like this on work time, but would you have a moment? I've been going through a rough time lately and could use some advice."

Martin felt uncomfortable by Rigby's sudden switch in tone and temperament. But he also felt a tendril of excitement, sensing an opportunity to make points with Rigby and, perhaps, use it as leverage to be in a position to pick an assistant or to stave off his own demise within the company if necessary.

"Take all the time you like." Martin stretched his arms over his head and clasped his hands behind his neck, a posture he often adopted in meetings to feign contentment with an unwanted or boring conversation. "I'm here to listen."

"That's kind of you, Martin. I know I don't have to ask, but this is strictly private between us."

"Of course ... what's said in here stays in here."

"I appreciate that. Well, it's my wife. We're thinking about a divorce. We haven't been getting along for awhile, and because we don't have children, it seems like nothing is holding us together except fighting. But still ..."

Martin could see that Rigby wanted him to finish the sentence, but he had no idea what to say. A sudden fluttering in his chest made him sit upright and lower his arms. Frightened, he pressed his fingers against his breastbone.

"Yes," Rigby said, coming to life. "It gets me there ... in the heart. I knew you would understand. That's why I wanted to talk to you. I know you've been through it."

The fluttering stopped and Martin eased his fingers away from his chest.

"And …" Rigby paused, flushing slightly. "I mean, it's not a terrible thing to be single again … even at our age?"

Martin got it now. Rigby wanted him to tell him how great it was to be divorced, to be dating, to be free and clear of the institution of marriage. He certainly thought this way years ago, when he and his wife first split, and he saw every beautiful woman as a potential soul mate. But the last few years had blunted that idea, and now, in terms of happiness, at least with his current girlfriend, all he wanted was peace and quiet.

"I won't lie to you," he said. "It's wonderful. There are more gorgeous women than you can count looking for a good man. You'll have your pick."

Rigby's face relaxed.

"That's what I hear. But it's hard to believe. I guess I'm old fashioned. I must take after my parents. They just celebrated their fiftieth anniversary. I know they'll be upset if my wife and I split up. How did you handle it?"

"Dating younger women?"

"No, telling your family about the divorce."

"Oh." Martin shrugged. "We're not that close. My mother passed when I was young, and my three sisters live far away. I do remember my father calling me up right after he found out to see if I needed anything. He even wanted to pay for my lawyer."

"I'll take him up on that," Rigby joked. "Divorce attorneys are expensive."

"Mine certainly was."

Martin shook his head, as if ruing the large law bill, when in actuality he was thinking about that phone call. He had been more angry than grateful by his father's offer, feeling as if he didn't think he could handle his own problems. He also had heard from one of his sisters that the old man was subsisting on a small, fixed income. But he knew that if he had said yes, that he needed the money, his father would have found a way to pay the tab. For some reason, this knowledge had made Martin feel even madder.

"Your father," Rigby said. "May I ask if he's still with us?"

"Alive? Oh, yes. I believe he's 83 … or is it 84? Somewhere around there."

"In good health?"

"Uh-huh," Martin said, although he was not exactly sure. The last time he had spoken to his father was close to two years ago. But he assumed if there was anything wrong one of his sisters would have told him.

"Good for him," Rigby said. "And for you if you inherited his genes."

Martin forced out a smile. In reality, he was very much like his father, physically. People always commented when he was growing up how much they looked alike: how they shared the same build, features, that they even walked the same way. He didn't mind it when he was young, but as he got older he began to resent the comparisons.

"I admire the older generation," Rigby continued. "To me they worked hard and didn't complain when things didn't go their way. Now everyone wants to get to the top right away. I can't tell you how many employees here think they can do the job better than the person above them. It's why I was disappointed to learn about Jillian. She's one of the few people in this company who never filed a grievance against their boss or came into my office to discuss a problem with another employee. And did you know she's never taken a sick day? Not one. That type of dedication and endurance is very rare."

"I pride myself on my work ethic as well," Martin said, feeling defensive. "Perhaps she followed my example. I'm never sick."

"I'm sure she did. Although last year, didn't you have troubles with your back? Does it still bother you?"

Martin had forgotten about the back. He had tweaked it one night, slipping on some ice outside a nightclub. It was not enough of an injury to slow him down, but he did use it as an excuse to take leave from work and go on vacation to the Bahamas.

"No, thankfully I'm perfectly fit and feeling well again."

"So you do take after your father. Sorry to be so curious, but may I ask what he did for a living?"

"My father worked for an apparel company."

"How interesting," Rigby said. "What was his job?"

"A little bit of everything, I suppose."

It was another lie. His father had been a maintenance worker in a shoe-making plant, a janitor. The totality of his duties were to sweep up between the assembly lines and take out the refuse. It was a non-union shop, so the pay wasn't great. But it was steady work and the salary covered the family's bills ... or at least whatever his father felt was essential. Which, in his case, meant they didn't own a car or even a television.

"My dad was a chef," Rigby said. "French-trained. He loved to cook."

Martin nodded. Now that Rigby had opened the floodgates, anything he said seemed to trigger a memory. Martin saw his father, youthful now, standing in front of the little stove in their home, making breakfast for him and his sisters, preparing sandwiches he would stuff in brown bags for them to take to school, rushing them to the door so they could make class on time, and then riding his bicycle to the plant three miles away. His father also cooked dinner for them, every night. Never once did they eat out as a family, not in all the years Martin lived at home.

"You can imagine how wonderful we had it," Rigby continued, patting his stomach. "I must say I felt very privileged growing up."

Martin felt just the opposite. Maybe it was being raised with only the basics, or without a mother, but he always felt somehow deprived as a child. It fueled his decision to live a different life once he got out and was on his own, a life filled with as much luxury and love as possible. He had succeeded in some ways with luxury. Despite the divorce and child support, his job paid enough that he owned a high-priced condo, an expensive car, dined at the best restaurants, splurged regularly on vacations. But love had proven elusive. His marriage had failed, he felt estranged from his daughter, and he was on the brink of breaking up with yet another girlfriend.

"I've taken up too much of your time," Rigby said, slapping his knees. "You can't imagine how helpful this has been. I don't even remember the last time I talked so much about things like this ... you know, man-to-man."

"I enjoyed it too."

"I hope you know, Martin, that even if my door is closed, it's open to you. You're always welcome to come in and talk about anything that's bothering you."

Martin smiled.

"Thankfully, all's good for me. But if I ever need anything, I'll take you up on it."

"Please do."

Martin watched Rigby leave. He was about to reach down for another pill when Jillian stuck her head into the office.

"Ms. Cohn called while you were meeting with Mr. Rigby. She wants to know if you can have lunch with her?"

Martin exhaled through his nose. Cohn was his direct supervisor. He knew she was waiting on him to provide some new ideas on how to jumpstart sales.

"Today?"

"Yes. She's suggested that new French place nearby."

"I see."

Jillian stepped in further.

"What would you like me to tell her?"

Martin hesitated.

"Is it any good?" he finally said. "The French place?"

"I wish I could tell you, but I always eat at my desk."

"Oh. Right."

"So ... Ms. Cohn?"

Martin hesitated again, looking at Jillian, suddenly feeling a vague sense of nostalgia ... or was it despair? He wasn't sure.

"I'd rather not with her," he said. "Perhaps you might join me for lunch? We'll go somewhere nice ... my treat."

Jillian blinked into the invitation.

"That's kind of you, sir, but I brought my lunch from home."

"Save it for dinner. You can have whatever you like today: shrimp, steak, lobster ... you name it."

"I'm sorry, sir, but I'll pass. I made an egg salad sandwich I really like. Besides, I don't want you to spend money on me."

"Don't be silly. Let's live a little."

"Please, don't let me stop you. You should go enjoy a nice lunch. I'm fine."

Martin began to get angry. He stared hard at Jillian. She wasn't making this easy.

"Don't you get it?" he snapped. "I don't want to eat with Ms. Cohn. Can't you forget your stupid brown bag this one time, throw your egg salad in the garbage and enjoy a decent meal?"

Jillian's face hardened.

"It's not in a brownbag, sir. My sandwich, it's in Tupperware. It keeps it fresh."

Martin tried to gather himself.

"Right, I was just making a point … about the need to enjoy yourself. You shouldn't worry about every penny. It's important to live for the moment, indulge in life's pleasures, because you never know what the future might hold. Remember that."

"I will, sir."

"I suppose then I'll have to eat with Ms. Cohn."

Jillian shook her head.

"I can call her back and say you left before I could tell you she wanted to meet with you. I'm happy to take the blame to help you out."

Martin looked at Jillian, genuinely puzzled.

"Why?" he said after a moment.

"Sir?"

"Why would you take the blame? Why are you always so happy to help me out, to do anything I ask, to never ask anything from me. Why?"

"Because it's my job."

"It's more than that," Martin said. "Everyone has a job, but not everyone is like you: not everyone is loyal, or dutiful, or even decent. What's wrong with you?"

Jillian blinked again. Martin thought he saw tears forming in her eyes.

"I'm sorry," he said. "I didn't mean to upset you. It's just a stressful time for me."

"I understand, sir. But things will get better. They always do."

"I appreciate that." He paused. "I appreciate you."

"Thank you, sir. Should I call Ms. Cohn now?"

"Please."

Martin watched as Jillian left the office. His anxiety, strangely, had lifted, replaced by a melancholy which made him feel sad but somewhat grounded. It was as if a heavy blanket had been wrapped around his shoulders, holding him down but also keeping him sheltered.

Jillian came back, smiling.

"Ms. Cohn said next week for lunch will work just as well."

"Thanks."

Jillian turned to leave the office.

"Jillian?"

"Yes?"

"Would you mind bringing your lunch in here? I mean, I'd like it if we could eat together today ... if that's okay with you?"

"If that's what you want, sir. Should I order you some takeout?"

Martin bowed his head a moment before looking back at Jillian

"Actually, I haven't had a homemade sandwich in a long time. Do you think I could have half of your egg salad?"

"Of course, sir," Jillian said, her face brightening. "I also have carrot sticks."

Jillian was not long away. When she came back she laid out the lunch picnic style on Martin's desk, making sure to give him a paper plate and several napkins along with a Styrofoam glass full of cold water. They ate mostly in silence, but it was not uncomfortable. In fact, Martin could not remember a more relaxing meal, listening to the sound of them chewing and swallowing, the hard crunching of the carrots.

After they finished, Jillian cleaned up and went back to her desk. An hour or so later, Martin heard her phone ring. She came in after to tell him she had to run down to Mr. Rigby's office. She asked if he needed her to bring him back anything. Martin, for the first time that day, told the truth: he needed nothing.

ACKNOWLEDGEMENTS

Two Syllable Men would not have been possible without the encouragement and affirmation of the editors who published earlier versions of these stories in their literary journals and magazines. These hardworking, talented and dedicated individuals include Anne James (*Zymbol*), Ben Evans (*Fogged Clarity*), Veronica Gorodetskaya (*The Capra Review*) and Mark Mirsky (*Fiction Magazine*). I am also indebted to Burt Weissbourd, a writer's writer, who read the collection and gave it a "thumbs up" when I truly needed it. Last, and most important, I would like to thank Jessica Bell at Vine Leaves Press for her enthusiastic support of the writing, and for giving this male character a chance to introduce 12 other male characters to readers.

VINE LEAVES PRESS

Enjoyed this book?
Go to *vineleavespress.com* to find more.

CPSIA information can be obtained
at www.ICGtesting.com
Printed in the USA
FFOW05n0245040416